"My unicorn
she exclaim

Sophie accepted the tiny glass
figure with a sigh of pleasure.
"You've given it back to me."

"It's bargaining power works
both ways." Angelo had turned
toward her.

"I don't know what you mean."

"Don't you?" He began to remove the
pins from her hair, letting each
strand cascade through his fingers.
"It's quite simple. The understanding
between us was that the unicorn
was a pledge that could be
redeemed for a favor. You asked one
of me, even though it may not have
turned out as you expected. Now it's
my turn to ask a favor of you."

She didn't need to ask what he
wanted. It was there—in the naked
hunger in his eyes as he slid down
the strap of her dress to bare her
shoulder for his lips.

Books by Sara Craven

These books may be available at your local bookseller.

Don't miss any of our special offers. Write to us at the following address for information on our newest releases.

Harlequin Reader Service
P.O. Box 52040, Phoenix, AZ 85072-2040
Canadian address: P.O. Box 2800, Postal Station A,
5170 Yonge St., Willowdale, Ont. M2N 6J3

SARA CRAVEN

promise of the unicorn

Harlequin Books

TORONTO • NEW YORK • LONDON
AMSTERDAM • PARIS • SYDNEY • HAMBURG
STOCKHOLM • ATHENS • TOKYO • MILAN

Harlequin Presents first edition February 1986
ISBN 0-373-10856-7

Original hardcover edition published in 1985
by Mills & Boon Limited

CHAPTER ONE

ALL the way up in the train, Sophie had been rehearsing what she meant to say, but now that she had actually arrived—found herself enclosed in the discreetly imposing surroundings of the foyer of the Marchese bank, her mind seemed to have become a complete blank.

Not that it mattered, she thought, her mouth twisting wrily. Judging by the polite but implacable treatment she had met with at the reception desk, her journey on which so much doubt, reluctance and heart-searching had been lavished, was going to be a wasted one.

'You wish to see *Signor* Angelo Marchese?' The receptionist's eyebrows had risen by a fraction, and her eyes had measured Sophie, taking in every detail of the expensively simple navy wool suit, and the white lawn blouse beneath it. 'Have you an appointment?'

In spite of herself, Sophie felt a faint blush rising. How could she possibly explain to this well-groomed Gorgon the sudden impulse which had brought her here? 'I'm afraid not,' she managed, adding quickly as she saw the other woman's mouth beginning to shape the negative. 'But if you could just tell him that—that Miss Ralston is here, and would be grateful for a moment of his time.'

'*I bet*' Sophie's sensitive antennae picked up

from the receptionist's silence, but the older woman merely said with cool civility, 'I'll tell his secretary, Miss—er Ralston, but I'm afraid I can't promise anything. Perhaps you'd like to take a seat over there.'

My God, Sophie thought as she turned away, grabbing at her poise. She thinks I'm one of Angelo's women. If it wasn't so nauseating, it would almost be laughable.

She could have put her right, of course. She could have said, 'Actually, *Signor* Marchese is my cousin by marriage.' But she didn't do so. It wasn't a relationship she had any desire to acknowledge. For years, it seemed, she had been fighting to hold on to her own identity, to avoid being absorbed, however kindly, into the Marchese clan. Ever since, in fact, her mother, a widow with a young daughter had married John Marchese.

John was a big, ebullient, warm man, prepared to dote uncritically on his new stepdaughter. It was true to say that there had been little Sophie had ever wanted in her eighteen years that John was not happy to give her.

Except the one thing that really matters, she thought with a sigh.

She glanced surreptitiously at her watch. She'd been sitting on this admittedly comfortable sofa in a corner of the foyer for nearly forty minutes. At first she'd felt self-conscious, now, she felt invisible. She supposed this was the ploy with unwanted callers—to leave them there until they gave up and crept ignominiously away.

But, I'm damned if I will, Sophie thought,

tilting her chin. I'm here now, and I'll stay until they have to carry me out. I'm never going to get such an opportunity to see Angelo again.

As the youngest ever chairman of the Marchese bank, Angelo spent a lot of his time jetting between the various capital cities of the world, and it was London's turn to suffer one of his periodic descents.

Even so, Sophie had not seriously considered seeking him out until she'd heard her stepfather mention casually over dinner the night before that he himself would be away from the bank for the entire day, attending some financial conference in the Midlands. It had really seemed to Sophie as if fate was giving her a nudge, and so she'd swallowed pride and misgivings alike, and caught the first train to London after breakfast.

And much good it had done her, she thought crossly. She might as well have stayed quietly at home, and relied on trying to snatch a private moment with Angelo when he attended her parents' wedding anniversary party in a few days time.

Except that would probably have been harder than trying to get to him here, she knew. Wherever Angelo visited, he was invariably the guest of honour, and there would be many people ahead of her in the queue to monopolise his attention, even for a few minutes.

Under normal circumstances, Sophie would have crossed streets to keep out of Angelo's way. At their first meeting nine years ago at her parents' wedding, she'd been frankly in awe of this tall, rather aloof young man with his aquiline features and hooded eyes. The Marchese bank had been lending money to the whole of Europe since the days of Lorenzo the Magnificent, and Sophie had no difficulty in translating Angelo into silks and velvets, with a pearl in his ear and a dagger in his hand, she thought vengefully.

And then, for a while, her view of him had changed, after the day he'd arrived unexpectedly at their country house at Bishops Wharton and found her crying on the terrace steps.

She couldn't even remember at this distance what her tears had been about. Probably her mother had sensibly put paid to some particularly blatant piece of spoiling on John's part, and she was bewailing the fact. And then suddenly Angelo was sitting beside her, regardless of moss, or dust or dead leaves, his arm round her, his voice calling her '*mia cara*' and asking what the matter was.

As if it was yesterday, she could remember the silky glide of his sleeve under her cheek as he comforted her, that indefinable air of arrogant command she had sensed subdued for once, as she sobbed out some halting explanation. Remembered, too, the faint scent of his cologne, a subtle musky fragrance he still used, although these days she took care not to get too close, and which had clung to the immaculate white handkerchief he had used to dry her tears.

If he'd been secretly amused by the desolate picture she presented, at least he'd kept it to himself. His usually cool drawl had been oddly gentle as he'd soothed her, telling her there was nothing in her world worth the shedding of a single tear, and that in a day or two she would have forgotten all about it. She'd sat in the circle of his arm, almost mesmerised by the sound of his voice, until at last, worn out with emotion, she'd fallen asleep.

And then, a few days later, a package had arrived addressed to her, and when she'd removed the layers of padded wrapping, she'd discovered to her delight a small glass unicorn, and a note.

She was a Marchese now, Angelo had written, and the unicorn was part of the Marchese family crest. In addition, it was a pledge between them. If Sophie would promise not to cry anymore over trifles, then, one day, when she found something she wanted with all her heart, she could return the unicorn to him, and he would help get it for her, if he could.

Barbara Marchese had disregarded the note, but her brows had risen when she looked at the unicorn Sophie held so proudly. 'John—it's Venetian glass, and terribly old. Is Angelo mad? Sophie will break it.'

'I don't think so.' John Marchese had fondly stroked his stepdaughter's fair hair. 'Will you, Sophie?'

Mutely, she'd shaken her head. Nor had she. She'd treasured the unicorn, and Angelo had become her god. She'd hero-worshipped him openly, trying vainly to think of something she wanted enough to fulfil the terms of their bargain, because it was so much like a fairy tale, and she wanted the magic to happen there and then.

But gradually, as the years passed, her attitude had changed again, as she began to perceive Angelo not as hero, but as a man, powerful, incredibly attractive and sexually charismatic, and started to make sense of the items she read in gossip columns about him.

She supposed she'd been unutterably naïve, but she'd been at boarding school a couple of years before she finally realised from the frank remarks of some of the senior girls exactly what Angelo's relationship was with these 'constant companions' who appeared and disappeared in his life with such monotonous regularity. And it had been a shock to find that her prince—her fairy godfather—was in fact avidly fancied by many of her contemporaries.

'Lucky Sophie,' Camilla Liddell had gloated. She was older than Sophie would ever be, with sleepy knowing eyes. 'Does beautiful cousin Angelo let little Sophie sit on his knee and cuddle him?' She'd smiled maliciously at Sophie's sudden flush, and added some suggestions which had made her skin crawl with disgust.

That night, in her cubicle, she'd cried herself to sleep, the covers over her head so as not to disturb the others, because something precious had been destroyed forever. And when she went home at half term, she'd almost expected to find the unicorn in shining fragments on the floor. It was some small consolation to find it still intact, but nothing was ever the same again. From that day onwards, she was on her guard, and as Angelo himself seemed to have withdrawn to a distance when they next met, the gulf between them had remained virtually unbridgeable ever since.

And that was why she'd hesitated so long about approaching him now, Sophie thought, winding a strand of her pale hair round her finger, as she often did when worried by something. Because it seemed the promise of the unicorn might have been made between two different people altogether—or, indeed, never happened at all—a figment of her childish imagination.

Except that the proof of it was there in her handbag—the unicorn itself, tissue-wrapped and tangible. But would he even remember it? And couldn't this attempt to enlist his help simply turn into another item on the long list of the times she'd made a fool of herself in front of Angelo?

She groaned inwardly. Maybe it would be better to yield to circumstances and creep away quietly.

'Sophie?' A man's voice, tinged with amazement. 'My dear, what on earth are you doing here? John isn't in today. Surely you knew that?'

Sophie glanced up, recognising Leonard Grant, who was deputy in her stepfather's department.

She swallowed, meeting his puzzled gaze. 'Actually, it was Angelo I wanted to see. I—I didn't realise I needed an appointment.'

Leonard gave her a sympathetic smile. 'Well, as you can imagine, the staff here have strict orders to keep pretty girls who come here asking for Angelo at bay. But that wouldn't apply to you. You're family, after all. Didn't you tell them that? Didn't John tell you what to do?'

'Er, no.' Sophie looked down at the tiled floor. 'As a matter of fact, he doesn't know I'm here. You see,' she added, improvising wildly. 'It's a secret—a secret about the anniversary party.'

'I see.' Leonard patted her shoulder. 'Well, in that case I'll have to see what I can do. I'm sure Angelo could spare you a moment, under the circumstances.'

She watched him go. Well, she was committed now. It was like getting on a roller coaster and wishing you hadn't, but knowing just the same there was no getting off.

Suddenly, she could hear Mark's voice in her ear, softly persuasive. 'Darling, the guy's your cousin, even if it is only by marriage. If anyone could help us, it's him. Is it really so much to ask?'

'Yes,' she thought despairingly. 'Far too much.' She wished she was a million miles away, and still travelling. But she wasn't here just for herself. She was here for Mark, for their happiness. Surely her love for him was worth the sacrifice of a little pride?

She sat on the edge of her seat, feeling as if only her tension was holding her together until Leonard came back. He was smiling.

'You're in luck. He was just about to go to lunch. I'll take you up to the top floor.'

She was so nervous she could hardly speak as they went up in the lift.

A dark girl was waiting for them, looking upset. She almost pounced on Sophie. 'Miss Ralston? I'm so sorry—I didn't realise. I haven't worked here for very long, and I didn't know you were a member of the family.'

Sophie wanted to reply, 'I'm not' but under the circumstances that would hardly be tactful, she realised, especially as the double doors standing open opposite the lift undoubtedly led straight into Angelo's office.

She was ushered in, heard the secretary's nervous, 'Miss Ralston, sir,' and felt the doors close behind her.

Her first impression was one of dazzle. Light poured into the penthouse office from windows on three sides. If it was a ploy to put clients at a disadvantage; then it certainly worked, Sophie thought, blinking.

In all that light, Angelo was darkness, from the top of the thick black hair, springing back from his forehead, down over the immaculate city suit to the subdued gloss of his handmade shoes.

'*Cara* Sophie. What an enchanting surprise.'

The words were welcoming, but there was mockery just below the surface, rasping along Sophie's nerve-endings. She looked at him numbly, unable to think of a single thing to say in reply. This was the effect he invariably had on her, she realised bitterly, wiping everything from her mind with the sheer power of his physical presence.

He began to walk towards her, moving with the lithe sinuous grace of a black panther, and Sophie felt the breath catch in her throat as she registered yet again, the sheer impact of his devastating good looks. It was unfair, she thought unwillingly, assimilating the long-lashed brilliance of his eyes, the high-bridged patrician nose and the proud sensual curve of his mouth.

He halted a few feet from her, lifting one eyebrow in a combination of enquiry and amusement. 'Lost for words, *cara*? Leonard tells me you wish to discuss some matter to do with the anniversary party—some problem, perhaps?'

Sophie swallowed. 'Well—not exactly,' she returned feebly. 'I know I did tell Leonard that, but actually it's something rather more personal.'

'I see.' The midnight eyes studied her for a long moment, then he turned away with a faint shrug. 'I think this may take rather longer than I thought. Forgive me for a moment.'

He walked to the long curved desk, and flicked a button on the intercom system. 'Miss Bradley? Telephone the Savoy, if you please, and make my excuses to *Signora* Vanni, and whatever apologies are necessary. Assure her that I look forward to our theatre engagement this evening.' He listened for a moment, as the message was being repeated, then nodded. '*Bene*. Perhaps you would also arrange for lunch for two to be served in the director's dining room. I understand it is not being used today.'

'Oh, please, no,' Sophie interrupted, mortified. 'There's really no need to go to all this trouble— change your arrangements like this. And I don't want lunch. I—I'm really not hungry.'

'Perhaps not, but I am.' His tone was faintly crushing.

'Yes, but you could still go to the Savoy. I could come back some other time . . .' Sophie began to back towards the door.

Angelo sighed impatiently. 'Please don't be foolish, Sophie. Presumably you had some important motive for seeking me out in this way. Has it suddenly become less so?'

Sophie bit her lip. 'No,' she admitted stiffly. 'Only, I didn't mean to intrude—to interfere in your personal affairs. I'm sorry.'

He gave a swift shrug. 'Don't be. Unless it is also your intention to disrupt my arrangements for this evening too?'

She flushed. 'Oh, no.' She stole a look at him beneath her lashes. 'Is the lady you're meeting Gianetta Vanni, the dress designer? I read in the papers she was in London.'

'It is,' he said briefly. 'But we are here to discuss some personal matters of yours, not mine.'

Sophie's flush deepened. That was the real Angelo, she thought. King of the cutting remark, making her feel a schoolgirl again. She wished she could tell him to go to hell.

He glanced at the thin platinum watch on his wrist. 'Lunch will be a few minutes. Perhaps you would like an *aperitivo*—something to calm your ruffled temper, and give you courage perhaps,' he added sardonically.

Sophie opened her eyes wide. 'Do I need courage?' she asked, deciding it was safer to overlook the remark about her temper.

The dark face was enigmatic suddenly. 'That, *cara*, will depend probably on the magnitude of the problem you wish to discuss with me. So— will you have a sherry, perhaps, or a martini?'

'Sherry would be fine.' Sophie sent him an angelic smile. 'Do you know this is the first time you've ever offered me a drink. Is it an acknowledgement that you regard me as an adult at last?'

His mouth twisted. 'No—merely that I recognise that in the eyes of the law at least, you are now old enough to be given alcohol—no more. Don't hope for too much from me, Sophie,' he added acidly.

Rage made her dumb as he crossed to an antique cabinet and extracted a decanter and two crystal glasses. The sherry was pale gold and very dry, and Sophie could cheerfully have thrown it all over him, but her reasons for seeking him out, allied with the certainty that he would undoubtedly retaliate if she did any such thing, stayed her hand. And, oddly enough, the sherry did seem to have a calming effect, its caress like velvet against the taut muscles of her throat.

As she sipped it and began slowly to look around her, and take in her surroundings, she was able to see that although it was a large room, it was far more businesslike and less luxurious than any of her previous imaginings about the Marchese bank had suggested. Not that she'd ever expended much thought on the subject, she hastily reminded herself, but it had always seemed natural to picture Angelo against a background of opulent marble halls.

But the only real sign of opulence in the room was the chair on which she herself was now seated. It was low, made from some pale hide, deeply cushioned, and designed, she realised to put anyone who used it at an actual physical disadvantage, staring up at the huge desk which dominated the room, and the dominating man who sat behind it.

As their glances met, he sent her a faint smile, and lifted his glass in salute. 'Well, Sophie?'

He wanted to know why she had come, and she didn't know what to say, or where to begin.

'Is this where you put people when they want a loan?' she asked at last, trying for brightness and playing for time.

'Sometimes.' The dark brows lifted mockingly. 'I hope you don't want to ask for a loan, Sophie.'

'Oh, no,' she said hastily, thanking her stars that it was true. She looked round her again, avoiding his gaze. 'What a fantastic building this is. Of course, I've never been here before.'

'But that,' Angelo reminded her silkily, 'is entirely through your own choice. I seem to remember when it was once suggested, you told me that all commerce was disgusting but bankers were the worst of all, because they were predators. Or had you forgotten?'

No, she hadn't forgotten. The memory still made her cheeks burn, particularly as she'd chosen a family dinner party for her outburst. It had been sparked off by a letter from a friend, Rosemary, blotched with tears to say that she wouldn't be returning to school the following term, because her father's company was in financial trouble. Rosemary had not had a complete grasp of what had happened, but it seemed clear her father was being made bankrupt, and they would lose nearly everything they possessed.

The letter had upset Sophie, and she'd tried to

discuss it with her mother, but Barbara, abstracted over her guests, had said, 'Later, darling.'

During the dinner, she'd been quiet, thinking of Rosemary, and her family, and the trouble which had come to them, and when she'd come out of her reverie, it was to find careers were being discussed, and that she was suddenly the focus of attention, with John proposing not too seriously that she might find an opening in the Marchese bank.

She'd looked past him and seen Angelo—seen the slightly derisive smile which twisted his mouth as he listened, and had exploded, the natural tension he inspired in her combining lethally with the anguish she felt for Rosemary. She had heard her voice storming into the startled silence, saying stupid, unforgivable things that she was totally unable to prevent, cringing from them, from the shock on John and Barbara's faces, and from the contempt in Angelo's eyes.

How typical of him to remind her, she thought stormily.

She said evenly, 'Are you still blaming me for something I said when I was a child?'

'Implying that you are now a woman?' Angelo's mouth curled.

He watched her react, as his tiny shaft struck home, then went on, 'And a woman who wants something. That's a dangerous combination, Sophie.'

She remained silent. Nothing about this interview was going as planned. The determination which had prompted her to seek it had vanished, and only the difficulties remained.

'We established, I think, that you did not wish to choose banking as a career,' the smooth voice went on. 'What have you decided to do with your life?'

She hesitated. Now was the time to tell him. He'd provided her with the perfect opening, but still she prevaricated. 'I'm starting a secretarial course in the autumn.' She tried a smile. 'I can't go on living at home forever, although I've enjoyed this year. John felt that I'd been away so much at school that it was time I got to know them both all over again.'

'You don't have to explain the situation to me.' He was lounging in his chair, watching her, his face giving nothing away. 'And shall you enjoy being a secretary?'

Sophie shrugged. 'It's an—adequate way of making a living,' she returned.

'And is that really so vital? You are now a rich man's daughter, do not forget.'

'Oh, there's no danger of that. After all, you'll always be there to remind me, won't you?'

He smiled lazily, 'Of course.' He paused, as a respectful knock at the door heralded lunch. 'Shall we go in?'

Sophie took a deep breath and struggled out of the chair, ignoring the helping hand he offered her. She felt oddly light-headed as she stood up. She'd been a fool to have that sherry on an empty stomach, she reproached herself as she allowed herself to be conducted out of the office and along the carpeted corridor to the directors' dining room.

It was a quite a small room, the oak-panelled

walls imposing an extra intimacy. A table had been set for them beside the window, with its view of roofs, glass tower blocks and steeples. The sun spilled across the spotless white damask cloth, and sparkled from the crystal and silverware. There were flowers, scented carnations in a silver vase, in the centre of the table, and wine cooling in a napkin covered container.

In spite of her nervousness, and her earlier claim that she wasn't hungry, Sophie found the scene irresistibly inviting. Besides, she hoped the food would put some fresh heart into her.

'Your jacket, miss?' An elderly waiter was hovering benevolently, waiting to take it from her. As Sophie twisted her body slightly, sliding her arms out of the sleeves, she saw that Angelo was watching her, his dark eyes frankly appraising the thrust of her breasts against the thin lawn blouse.

She tried to return his glance with cool indifference, but she was already aware of the mounting colour in her cheeks, and his scarcely veiled amusement at her embarrassment. It would have given her the greatest pleasure to have been able to walk out on him, she thought furiously.

She sat stiffly while the waiter served the avocado vinaigrette, wondering if she would be able to choke any of it past the knot of tension in her throat. She was remembering various laughing comments from her stepfather about Angelo's predilection for beautiful girls, and while she didn't consider she came into that category, it was nevertheless disturbing to be looked over in that way.

By coming here today, she'd placed herself at a disadvantage, she realised ruefully. It might have been safer to wait for the anniversary party, and approach him under the sanctuary of her stepfather's roof. As it was, she felt rather out on a limb suddenly.

It was all too easy to contemplate Angelo's wealth and power as chairman of the bank, and virtual head of the Marchese family, and to overlook the fact that he was also very much a man, barely more than thirty, and sensationally attractive.

And for the first time he'd looked at her, not as if she was a troublesome child, but as though he liked what he saw. She wished wryly that she'd stayed with the jeans and sweatshirts he was accustomed to from her.

The second course—chicken in a thyme and lemon sauce—was served, and the wine was poured. With a dignified, 'Perhaps you'll ring for me, sir, when you've finished,' the waiter withdrew.

'Alone at last,' Angelo remarked. 'Don't look so apprehensive, *cara*. There's a very solid table between us, and you have an assortment of cutlery with which to defend yourself should my wicked desires prove uncontrollable.'

Sophie addressed herself to her chicken, her face wooden, raging inwardly that he could apparently read her thoughts with such accuracy.

'No comeback?' he continued tauntingly. 'From your earlier remark, I thought you wanted me to regard you as a woman, but perhaps you're having second thoughts about that.'

The moment of truth had come. Sophie lifted her chin and gave him a cool look. 'Not in the slightest,' she countered. 'As it happens, it's all to the good if you're prepared to admit I'm not a child any more. You see——' she moistened her suddenly dry lips with the tip of her tongue. 'You see—I want to be married.'

CHAPTER TWO

THERE was a brief silence, blank, almost stunned, then Angelo burst out laughing.

'Is that a proposal, *mia cara*? If so, I'm more flattered than I can say, but it is more usual, you know, for the man to do the asking.'

'Of course it's not a proposal.' Sophie glared at him, stormy colour flaring in her face. 'I wouldn't marry you if . . .' She paused belatedly, realising her denial could have been more politely worded.

'If I were the last man left on earth?' Angelo supplied silkily. 'Why not have the courage of your convictions, Sophie, and say what you are undoubtedly thinking. So—let us agree that neither of us would be the choice of the other. Presumably you have met a man who meets all your stringent criteria as a husband. I am happy for you. Is that what you wanted to hear. Did you come here today to ask my blessing?'

'Not entirely.' Sophie fidgeted with her fork. She said carefully, looking down at her plate. 'You see, my parents don't want me to marry him, and I'm hoping you will persuade them to change their minds.'

There was another silence. She peeped at him under her lashes, and saw that he was frowning.

'You are of legal age, Sophie. Why do you need their consent?'

'Because of Grandfather Ralston's will,' she said baldly. 'Look, I'd better explain everything from the beginning.'

'I think you should.' He refilled her glass.

'I met Mark in the village a few months ago,' she said. 'I was caught in a shower of sleet, and I went into the antique shop in Market Street to shelter. It belongs to Mark's aunt, and he was looking after it for her while she went to some sale or other. Well, we got talking, and he made some coffee, and . . .' Sophie paused. 'Well, that's how it started,' she said flatly. 'We—fell in love.' She gave him a challenging look. 'Nothing to say?'

He shrugged. 'The story seems conventional and innocuous enough. What is your parents' objection?'

Sophie hesitated again. This was the difficult part. 'As it happens, Mark hasn't got a job. At least, he's had a couple since he left university, but they haven't worked out. Now, he has the most marvellous chance to go in with a man he knows called Craig Jefferson, making software for computers. He's been offered a partnership, a share in the business, but, of course, he has to buy it and . . .'

'And he has no capital,' Angelo finished for her. She saw his frown had deepened. 'I hope he has not tried to borrow money from John.'

'Oh, no.' Sophie shook her head quickly. 'There's no need. You see, there's the Ralston money that Grandfather left me. It isn't a great deal in your terms, but it would be enough to give Mark the start he needs. Only Grandfather was a real dyed in the wool male chauvinist. I only inherit the money when I'm twenty-one, or if I marry before that with the consent of my parents.'

'Which they will not give.' It was a statement not a question. 'They can hardly be blamed, *cara.*'

'You're as bad as they are.' Sophie bit her lip. 'I've heard all the arguments over and over again, and they don't matter. Mark and I love each other, and I want to do this for us. I want to give him the Ralston money and give him a start in life.'

He said drily, 'It is more usual for a man contemplating marriage to provide his own start. But I'm sure John has already made this point to you.'

'Many times,' said Sophie defiantly. 'And it makes no difference.'

'I imagined it did not,' he murmured. 'So— you have come to me. Why do you think I should recommend this—Mark as a suitable husband for you?'

'Because of a promise you once made.' Sophie fumbled for her bag, pulling out the tissue wrapped parcel with fingers that shook. 'You said if there was ever anything I really wanted—all I had to do was return it to you.' She unwrapped the unicorn and stood it on the table between them, where the sunlight turned it to fire. 'or are you going to tell me now that it was a piece of childish foolishness—something to keep me quiet, and that you didn't really mean a word of it?'

There was a long silence, then he said expressionlessly, 'If I said it, then I meant it. Be in no doubt of that.'

'Then you promised you'd help me obtain my heart's desire.' Sophie's pulses were beating strongly and heavily, and she was conscious of an odd film of perspiration on her brow suddenly.

Angelo's dark eyes were fixed on her broodingly, a strange harshness in their depths, giving the impression he wasn't really seeing her at all. He didn't answer at once, and she repeated breathlessly, 'You'll help me?'

He leaned forward, and picked up the unicorn. For an instant, it seemed as if the long, lean fingers were going to crush it into splinters, and Sophie watched in a kind of bemused horror, then the moment passed, and perhaps, after all, it had only been a figment of her imagination, because he was smiling at her easily, and slipping the little figurine into his pocket.

'As I promised, *cara*, you shall have whatever you most desire.' He paused. 'That is—if you are sure you know what it is?'

'I'm sure,' she said huskily. 'I love Mark. We love each other. And he deserves this chance. My parents are just prejudiced against him for nothing. They don't really know him.'

'Then improving their acquaintance must clearly be a priority,' Angelo said lightly. 'Now, finish your lunch, Sophie, or William will be angry with us.'

Her chicken had cooled rapidly, but she didn't care. She felt so exultant that she could have eaten sawdust and tasted only ambrosia. In the end, it had been easy, she told herself. He had remembered, after all, and he was going to keep his word.

He had also, she realised regretfully, kept the little unicorn, which she hadn't intended at all.

William reappeared, with offers of dessert which Sophie refused, opting for coffee alone. She sat impatiently, watching Angelo peel himself a peach, the strong brown fingers moveing deftly. She wished that lunch was over and she could make an excuse and leave. She wanted to get back to Bishops Wharton, and tell Mark the fantastic news.

When William had served the coffee and brought Angelo a cognac, he departed, and they were alone once more.

Sophie cleared her throat. 'So—how will you go about it then? Convincing my parents, I mean?'

He shrugged, watching the swirl of cognac in his glass. 'I haven't decided yet, but naturally, I wish to meet your Mark. I should only be a fool if I urged your marriage to someone I had never seen in my life. Will he be at the anniversary party, or has he been forbidden the house?'

'Oh, no,' Sophie said. 'I'm allowed to see him. It's just the idea of marriage that they're so against.'

'It is hardly surprising.' His tone was dry. 'Why not be patient, Sophie? Why not wait until you are twenty-one as your grandfather's bequest states?'

'I can't. If we wait much longer, Craig Jefferson's going to find himself another partner, and Mark will have missed out on the chance of a lifetime.'

'On the chance of a partnership, certainly,' Angelo agreed. 'But, does it have to be that? Are there no other positions with the company? A different starting point, perhaps, from which he can make his own way without the help of his bride's legacy.' He paused. 'I presume you have told him about the Ralston money?'

'Naturally. I have no secrets from Mark.'

'Admirable,' he said sardonically. 'And was it his idea to approach me for help, once you'd told him of the rash promise I gave you with the unicorn?'

'Er, no.' Sophie had to tread warily again. Mark's actual suggestion had been far more direct and basic. *The guy's loaded, sweetie. Couldn't you persuade him to lend you the money?* A suggestion she had flinched from. It had only been afterwards that she'd remembered the glass unicorn, and wondered if it might be a way out of their difficulties. 'Actually, it was all my own doing. Mark hasn't the least idea that I intended to approach you.'

'And presumably, if he had known of your intentions, he would have moved heaven and earth to stop you.'

She hated that undertone of sarcasm. 'Why should he?'

Angelo shrugged. 'Perhaps—because I am not noted for offering favours. And perhaps because he might be frightened I might take—advantage of you.'

There was another silence, and Sophie's

discomfort deepened. Mark had frowned when she'd tried to explain about her fraught relationship with Angelo.

'For heaven's sake, Sophie,' Mark had exclaimed impatiently. 'Don't you know you can't afford to upset men in his position. If you'd played your cards right, you could have had him eating out of your hand by now. He's not exactly immune to beautiful girls, you know.'

Snapping her attention back to the present, she said quickly, 'I don't suppose it even crossed his mind. Mark trusts me implicitly.'

'He sounds a paragon,' Angelo murmured. 'I shall be interested to see who has managed to awaken such a passion of devotion in you, if nothing else.'

Sophie set down her coffee cup with an indignant rattle. 'What do you mean by that?'

He smiled faintly, his eyes lingering in the wide eyes, then down to the vulnerable curve of her mouth. 'That in spite of your protests, you are still very much a child, Sophie, and that marriage is a drastic way to achieve maturity. Why don't you enjoy your first love for what it is, and forget marriage for a while?'

Sophie bit her lip as she rose to her feet, reaching for her jacket. 'That's exactly the sort of cynical remark I'd expect from you. I hope you're not suggesting that I should follow your example, and have one *affaire* after another.'

'On the contrary.' Angelo had risen too. He was standing, his head thrown back slightly, watching her, his face speculative. 'But I hope in turn that you have not fallen in love with this

young man because he is the first one to have
kissed you. That is hardly a sound basis for
matrimony.'

Sophie's face burned as she struggled into her
jacket. 'That's none of your business.'

He said flatly, 'You have made it my business.'
He walked round the table towards her. 'And the
least I can do, Sophie *mia*, is provide you with
grounds for comparison.'

She wanted to run, but the chair was behind
her, blocking her way, and as she tried to thrust it
from her path, Angelo reached her, his long arms
pulling her effortlessly against him.

She said hoarsely, 'Don't you dare to . . .' but
the remainder of her words were lost beneath the
pressure of his mouth on hers.

He was very strong, some part of her brain
acknowledged numbly. Under the elegant suit,
his body was like whipcord, and the kiss should
have been hard too. But it wasn't. Instead his lips
were warm and devastatingly sensuous as they
explored her own, coaxing them apart to provide
him with a more intimate access to her mouth.

Her mind was repeating 'No' over and over
again, but her mouth was surrendering, her body
melting against his, here in this sunlit cage of a
room.

He wasn't even holding her any more. His
hands were caressing her instead, stroking the
nape of her neck under the smooth fall of her
hair, tracing the curve of her spine beneath her
jacket, his fingers scorching her flesh through the
thin material of her blouse.

She could have stepped back away from him,

only she didn't, because suddenly she wanted the kiss to go on. And she knew too that she wanted him to go on touching her too. That she wanted to know how his hands would feel on her bare skin.

Sanity returned like a drenching with cold water, shattering the sensual dream world which had so insidiously enfolded and enticed her. She wrenched herself free, a hand going instinctively to cover the aroused fullness of her parted lips.

A voice she hardly recognised as her own, said, 'You had no right to do that.'

He shrugged, his eyes bright and merciless as they studied her. 'What right did I need? You are not this Mark's wife, Sophie, not yet.'

She said unsteadily, 'But I will be. And if I tell him what you've done . . .'

'Ah.' He smiled. 'But you won't tell him, will you, *cara*? Or, if you do, you won't tell the whole truth. Just as you didn't share the secret of the unicorn with him.'

His shrewdness appalled her. She flung back her head. 'I would never lie to Mark.'

His brows rose. 'So—what will you tell him? That it began with a kiss, and ended with both of us wanting more—much more.' He added softly.

Colour flared in her face. She said thickly. 'You're disgusting.'

'I'm honest,' he said cynically. 'But you, *mia cara*, are a little hypocrite, denying the responses of your own body.' He took a step towards her, his smile deepening. 'Shall I prove it to you?'

She recoiled, almost stumbling in her haste. 'Don't touch me.'

He halted. The dark eyes met hers, holding them effortlessly in thrall, and to her dismay she felt a shock of totally physical desire shiver through her body. He didn't have to touch, or even speak. The invitation was there in the way he was looking at her, and it would be easy, so fatally easy to cross the brief space which separated them, and answer that invitation with her lips, and her body.

She closed her eyes, blotting him out, rejecting him with her mind, a shudder of self disgust quivering through her.

But at least she was back in control again, and her eyes opened, unleashing at him all the scorn she could muster. She said quietly, 'You're despicable, and I wish with all my heart that I'd never come here.'

'Ah, but you did,' he said softly. 'And the bargain between us still stands, Sophie *mia*.'

She said violently, 'Well, I want no further part of it,' and, turning, walked away out of the room and away from him, wishing that her dignity would allow her to run.

By the time the train pulled in to Bishops Wharton, Sophie was almost able to convince herself that she'd been drunk. There was no other explanation for her behaviour. She'd had that sherry, and then he'd kept topping up her glass with wine, and she wished she knew a word bad enough to call him.

She went straight round to Market Street. Miss Langton was in the shop, and she gave Sophie an indifferent nod as the shop bell tinkled.

'He's in the flat,' she advised briefly. 'Go on up.'

As Sophie obeyed, she wondered about Mark's relationship with his aunt. As far as she could gather, each was the only relative the other had, yet there didn't seem to be a great deal of mutual affection. And when she'd tentatively asked Mark if his aunt couldn't lend him the money for the Jefferson partnership, he'd stared at her as if she was crazy.

'Aunt Edwina?' He'd laughed. 'Darling, that glorified junk shop of hers doesn't provide that kind of income.'

Sophie didn't argue, but she wondered whether Mark wasn't too dismissive of his aunt's business. The shop was always attractive and well-stocked, and Miss Langton appeared to have a shrewd knowledge of the value of each and every item.

Mark was stretched out on the sofa, watching television, but he sat up eagerly as Sophie came in.

'Darling.' He drew her down to him and kissed her, his lips lingering on hers. 'God, you look beautiful—like a million dollars.'

She smiled rather tautly, and sat down beside him. 'While we're on the subject of money, I went to see Angelo Marchese today.'

'You did?' Mark almost yelped. 'You wonderful girl. What did he say? Is he going to help us?'

'Up to a point.' Sophie chose her words carefully. 'He wants to meet you, and after that, hopefully, he's going to talk my parents round about our marriage.'

'Fantastic.' Mark hugged her, his face jubilant. 'So all I have to do is convince him I'm a solid citizen, and worth a boost in the right direction. Consider it done.' He shook his head at her. 'And you didn't want to approach him.'

'I still wish I hadn't.' Sophie stared down at the carpet. 'He made a pass at me.'

'Well, I'm not surprised,' Mark said cheerfully. 'You look delectable. I can hardly keep my hands off you myself,' he added with a ferocious leer.

Sophie didn't smile. 'Don't you care?' she asked curiously.

He sighed almost impatiently. 'Of course I care, darling, but I don't suppose it was any big deal. You're a member of his family now, after all. Besides, according to the papers, he has bigger fish to fry,' he added carelessly. 'Some dress designer woman. There was a picture of them at some nightclub last night.' Mark slid his arm round her shoulders. 'Now, tell me everything Marchese said.' He paused. 'I don't suppose he mentioned lending you the money.'

'No, he didn't,' Sophie said. 'And I could never ask him, Mark. Please believe that.'

'All right.' He gave a faint shrug. 'We'll play it the way you want it, darling. It seems to have worked pretty well up to now. What did you do? Appeal to his better nature?'

'I don't think he has one,' Sophie said bitterly. 'No, I—I reminded him that he'd been kind to me when I was a child—that's all.'

He grinned. 'Well, it was certainly enough.'

More than enough, Sophie thought bitterly. It

disturbed her that Mark seemed to have failed to understand her feelings in all this. He regarded the events of the day as some kind of unqualified triumph, as if all their difficulties had been swept away in one fell swoop.

Sophie, however, was far from sure about this. She had no doubt that Angelo could persuade her stepfather to do almost anything he chose—if he wished, but he had made no actual guarantees.

She said slowly, 'Mark, perhaps it would be safer not to hope for too much.'

'Nonsense,' Mark said briskly. 'Can't you see, darling, that just to meet someone of Angelo Marchese's stature is the biggest break I've ever had. It's the kind of chance I've dreamed of.'

Sophie gave him an uneasy glance. 'Still, maybe it would be better not to say anything yet to Craig Jefferson.'

He shrugged. 'Probably not.' He smiled at her. 'Who knows? If I play my cards right, maybe I won't need Jeffersons any more anyway.'

Her alarm deepened. 'What do you mean?'

He sighed. 'Oh, come on, Sophie. If it comes to a choice between Jeffersons and—say—the Marchese bank, then it's no contest. Even you must be able to see that.'

'But there is no choice,' Sophie protested, beginning to feel desperate. Mark seemed to be disappearing out of sight suddenly.

'Not yet. But then I haven't met your cousin.' Mark said almost absently. 'When and where is this meet to take place? Should I ring the bank? Make an appointment?'

Sophie sighed. 'No—you'll meet him at my

parents' anniversary party. And he's not my cousin,' she added sharply.

He gave her an indulgent smile. 'Don't quibble, sweetheart. And do cheer up. After all, this is exactly what we wanted.'

'It's what you wanted certainly,' Sophie said coolly. She rose, smoothing a non-existent crease in her skirt with hands that shook a little. 'I just hope we don't live to regret it.'

She felt no happier on the night of the anniversary party itself. She'd been on edge all day, but trying to hide it as she helped Barbara and Mrs Curzon the housekeeper to complete the final touches.

She was dreading the moment when she would have to face Angelo again. The memory of that shameful kiss he had inflicted on her was still strong, and she was unable either to laugh it off as unimportant, or shrug it away as experience. In fact, she was in danger of becoming obsessive about it, she told herself. And the most galling reflection was that Angelo would undoubtedly be highly amused if he knew of her heartsearchings over such a triviality.

She was in her room when his car swept up the drive. She caught a glimpse of the chauffeur opening the back of the Rolls, and his dark figure emerging, before whisking herself away from the window. The last thing she wanted was for him to look up and catch her peeping at him like a schoolgirl.

She took all the time in the world to bathe and dress for the party, timing her descent to the drawing room to coincide with Mark's arrival.

She took a long look in the mirror, and nodded with qualified approval. The new dress in white chiffon with its draped Grecian bodice and floating skirt was becoming, and she hoped her hair, piled into a carefully casual top-knot gave her some added sophistication.

Mark was standing before the appletree-log fire which had been kindled on the drawing room's wide hearth. He looked unfamiliar in the formality of his dinner jacket, and endearingly apprehensive as he glanced towards the door. Sophie went into his arms like a homing bird, lifting her mouth for his kiss.

'God, you look beautiful,' he said huskily.

She smiled up at him. 'We aim to please,' she whispered teasingly.

He swallowed. 'Is he here?'

She nodded. 'He arrived about a couple of hours ago,' she said neutrally.

'Has he said anything?'

Sophie bit her lip. 'I—er—I haven't seen him yet,' she offered rather weakly. 'I was upstairs when he arrived and . . .'

Mark groaned. 'I suppose you're avoiding him,' he accused. 'Sophie, for heaven's sake. We need to be nice to the man, and that includes you.'

'Fine,' she said tautly. 'Just how nice would you like me to be? I'm sure he'll meet me more than halfway.'

'Darling,' he said patiently. 'You're very innocent in many ways. Are you sure you didn't just—misinterpret an avuncular gesture?'

'Perfectly,' Sophie said. 'Any uncle who behaved like that could end up in court.'

He gave her a coaxing smile. 'My poor love, you sound as if you had quite a shock. But you're quite safe. I'll take care of you.'

It was what she wanted to hear, and as his arms closed round her again, she melted eagerly against him, closing her mind to everything but the realisation that this was Mark who she loved and who loved her . . .

From the doorway, Angelo said drily, '*La disturbo?* Am I disturbing you?'

Mark released her hurriedly, and Sophie stepped back, her face flaming, avoiding Angelo's ironic gaze as he came slowly across the room towards them.

He said coolly, 'Allow me to introduce myself. I am Angelo Marchese, and I think you must be the young man Sophie intends to marry.'

'I'm Mark Langton, yes.' While they shook hands, Sophie sought to recover her composure.

'I must apologise for my thoughtless intrusion,' Angelo was saying pleasantly. 'But I did not expect to find the drawing room occupied. *Sono molto dispiacente.*'

Mark said eagerly, 'It really doesn't matter. After all, the main purpose of my being here is to meet you.'

Angelo's eyes rested on his meditatively. 'As you say,' he agreed. 'Perhaps we could further our acquaintance over a drink? Sophie—will you act as hostess for us. I'll have whisky with ice if you please.'

'And with soda for me,' Mark put in, and Sophie noted irritably that his tone was almost deferential.

She said expressionlessly, 'Of course' and went off to get the drinks. When she returned Mark was in full spate about Craig Jefferson's company and the amazing opportunity for investment it presented, while Angelo listened with courteous interest. Mark broke off almost reluctantly to accept the drink she handed him.

Angelo lifted his glass to her. 'You are an enchantment to the eyes, *mia cara*,' he said softly. He looked at her empty hands. 'You don't drink with us. Not even a sherry—or perhaps—a glass of wine?'

Sophie shook her head, her eyes meeting his unflinchingly. 'I don't think alcohol agrees with me,' she said.

Angelo's eyes narrowed mockingly, but he made no reply, and at that moment John and Barbara came into the room, Barbara exclaiming distractedly because they had not been the first downstairs.

After that, the evening seemed to merge into a blur for Sophie. At the dinner table, she was nowhere near either Mark or Angelo and couldn't hear what, if anything, they were saying to each other.

And when the meal was over, she had to do the dutiful rounds of the other guests before she could ask her mother tentatively if she knew where Mark was.

Barbara frowned. 'He and Angelo seem to be smoking cigars in the conservatory,' she said tartly. 'I hope that young man doesn't mean to be a nuisance and monopolise Angelo for the remainder of the evening. He seems to be following him about, and as he's your guest, it's up to you to see that he behaves. I don't want Angelo to be annoyed.'

'Oh, God forbid,' Sophie's chin lifted. 'It doesn't occur to you, Mother, that they might have mutual interests to discuss this evening?'

Mrs Marchese gave her a dry look. 'Frankly, no, darling. Now please rescue Angelo. After all, he comes down here to relax.'

'Oh, really?' Sophie was openly sarcastic. 'I thought he had *Signora* Vanni for that.'

Barbara's expression was scandalised. 'Sophie—that is no concern of yours.'

Sophie shrugged wearily. 'Of course not. I'm sorry. I'll—go and break up the smoking party.'

But as she moved along the covered walk to the conservatory, Mark was already coming to meet her, his face alight, and his eyes gleaming with excitement.

'There you are.' He grabbed her arm, bruising the flesh. 'I've got to talk to you.'

Sophie detached herself, rubbing her arm ruefully. 'Is this private enough?' she asked, indicating the long cane seat which stood against the wall.

'Yes, of course.' He said down with her. 'Sophie, you're all wrong about Angelo Marchese. He couldn't have been nicer to me. He thinks, like me, that Craig's offer is the chance of a lifetime.' He paused, drawing breath. 'He says that I have ambition, and he likes that,' he disclosed with a kind of awe. 'He wants to get to know me better—discuss my future in more depth—his own words.' He took both her hands in his. 'Sophie, he's invited both of us to stay with him on this private island he has. He wants us to join him there at the end of the month.' He paused again. 'What do you think of that?'

She moistened her lips with the tip of her tongue. 'Angelo has invited you—us to Avirenze? I don't believe it.'

'Why not?' Mark's tone held a touch of aggression. 'I just told you—we got on well together.' He grinned. 'And I have the distinct impression he means to make me an offer himself.'

'An offer you can't refuse?' Sophie asked with a kind of desperate flippancy, then sobered. 'Mark—do we have to accept this invitation?'

'Of course we do.' He stared at her as if she was mad. 'A millionaire's hideout near Capri—that's fantasy stuff, and I'm not missing out. It's different for you,' he added a shade peevishly. 'I suppose you've been there a dozen times already.'

'No,' she said. 'I never have. My parents go each year, but they were always invited during term time.' She gave a wry smile. 'I can understand why, I suppose. I was enough of a brat to have started asking embarrassing questions about why Angelo was there with a different lady each time.'

'Was he?'

Sophie's brows lifted. 'You sound envious,' she accused with a smile in her voice.

But Mark didn't seem to hear the smile. He said flatly, 'Don't be ridiculous. Is this why you don't want to go to Avirenze? Because of some silly childhood embargo?'

She shook her head. 'Of course not. But I don't understand this invitation, and I can't really believe it's all as simple and friendly as you seem to think.' She took a breath. 'What it boils down to is—I don't like Angelo, and I don't trust him either.'

'Oh for God's sake, you're letting your prejudices run away with you,' Mark said irritably. 'This is important to me, Sophie, and important to my career. Hell, after we're married, we'll have to entertain clients, and you're not going to like them all, but you're going to have to behave as if you do. Well, start practising with your cousin Angelo.'

'Angelo is not my cousin,' Sophie reminded him wearily. 'And he's not noted for his philanthropy either.'

Mark shrugged. 'He agreed to help you when you asked him, didn't he,' he demanded unarguably. 'Anyway, I don't know what you're complaining about. A couple of weeks in the sun off the coast of Italy. Where's the harm in that?'

The harm, Sophie thought, was Angelo—the shadow in that sun. But it was clearly pointless pursuing any such argument with Mark. She'd seen Angelo's charm in operation before, and although she was immune, Mark was bound to be flattered by the attention he was receiving.

She said quietly, 'If you're really set on going, I suppose I must agree.'

'Sophie—don't act like a martyr,' he appealed with an irritated groan. 'This could be a turning point in our lives.' He kissed her. 'It will be wonderful,' he whispered. 'I know it will.'

She made herself smile, return his kiss, but the warmth of his lips did little to dispel the chill of unease within her—the chill that reminded her that the Marchese family had been manipulating people since the time of the Doges of Venice.

The party didn't break up until nearly three in the morning. It had been a great success, and people were leaving with obvious reluctance.

Mark was among the first to go. 'I don't want to out-stay my welcome,' he murmured as he kissed her goodbye. 'After all, I want your family to like me.'

Sophie was troubled, however, as she made her way back to the drawing room. John and Barbara had been little more than civil all evening, and she could imagine their reaction when they learned Mark was going to Avirenze. If Angelo's ploy was to force Mark into their company, then it clearly wasn't going to work, and so she would tell him.

But finding an opportunity to do so was another matter. Angelo was deep in conversation with her stepfather, and they looked as if they might be there for the rest of the night, so at last, she admitted defeat, and said good night to the room at large.

But once in her bedroom she made no attempt to get undressed. She felt too jittery to rest or relax, and she sat by the window for a while, watching the stars fade.

It seemed ages before she heard the sounds of movement and muted voices which suggested the party had broken up at last.

She waited until the house was quiet, then slipped out of her room like a little ghost and made her way to the room Angelo occupied when he stayed with them.

She knocked, but there was no reply, and she hesitated. Surely, he couldn't be asleep already. She went to knock again, but as she did so, the door opened abruptly, and she was caught off-balance, her hand raised, feeling foolish.

She said lamely, 'Oh, there you are.'

'Where else did you imagine I would be at this hour?' Angelo returned drily. 'What do you want, Sophie?'

'I need to talk to you.'

'Then could it be at a more civilised hour? As you see, I was about to go to bed.'

Yes, she saw. He was wearing a dressing gown in dark red silk, reaching to mid-thigh and loosely belted at the waist. The neck hung open in a deep vee, revealing an expanse of hair-darkened skin. and the long muscular legs were bare too. His black hair looked damp and slightly ruffled, as if he's just taken a shower.

His eyes surveyed her impatiently. 'Well?'

'I'm sorry, but I'd rather it was now,' Sophie said. 'I—I won't keep you long.'

'That,' he said grimly. 'I can guarantee.'

As he motioned her past him into the room, and turned to close the door, Sophie knew a twinge of misgiving.

'Perhaps it would be better if I waited . . .' she began.

She saw the familiar gleam of mockery in the dark eyes. 'Nervous, Sophie? But of what? Surely not me—but perhaps—yourself?'

She flushed dully. 'That is not what I came here to discuss,' she said icily.

'How disappointing,' he said, and for a moment, the dark eyes rested on her lips like a disturbing caress.

She felt the breath catch in her throat, and hurried into speech. 'Why have you asked us to Avirenze?'

His brows lifted. 'I understood from your parents, it had always been one of your ambitions to go there.'

'When I was a child, perhaps.' Sophie said with hauteur.

'But no longer?' The long brown fingers cupped her chin, turning her reluctant face up to his. 'What is your objection?'

Sophie trod carefully. 'Because there's no need for you to go to these lengths. I know I asked for your help, but . . .'

'You did,' he said. 'And now you are questioning the way in which that help is to be given. Isn't that a little churlish, Sophie?'

Well, she should have expected that, Sophie thought grimly. She said, 'I thought you intended to encourage my parents to get to know Mark.'

'I do,' he said. 'And how better than during a relaxing stay on Avirenze. It's a very small island, Sophie *mia*. It encourages intimacy—at all levels.'

He was baiting her, but she refused to rise to it. A lot of the wind had been taken out of her sails anyway. 'You mean—Mother and John are coming as well. I—I didn't realise.'

'Naturally they will be there,' Angelo said. 'Anything else would hardly be decorous.'

'Oh?' Sophie's voice was tart. 'I wasn't aware that decorum was any big deal with you.'

He sent her a sardonic grin. 'But where members of my family are concerned,' he said softly. 'It will amaze you how decorous I can be.'

'I'm not a member of your family. I'm a Ralston,' she said flatly. 'Will other people be there too?'

His grin widened. 'Plenty of other people,' he said silkily. 'With a little care, *cara*, it should be possible for you to avoid me completely.'

She flushed mutinously. 'Will Gianetta Vanni be among them?' She could have bitten out her tongue the moment the question was asked. She expected a crushing snub in return.

But, all he said, quite mildly, was, 'You wish me to supply a guest list for your approval, *cara*?'

'No,' she snapped, hating him. 'It's your island. I suppose you're entitled to invite anyone you like.'

He laughed. 'Graciously spoken. So—have I allayed your fears? Do you still believe that I am willing to help you to your heart's desire?'

The words were lightly spoken, but she was aware that he was watching her keenly, and she moved awkwardly, avoiding his gaze.

At last, she said stiltedly, 'I'm sorry. I'm clearly putting you to a great deal of trouble.'

'You talk nonsense,' he said. 'And it was always my intention to invite you to Avirenze, *cara*.' He added softly. 'I was only waiting for you to become a woman.'

There should have been some smart comeback to that, but for the life of her, Sophie couldn't think of one.

Instead, she heard her voice sounding very young, and rather breathless, as she bade him good night and turned, heading blindly for the door.

He was there ahead of her, opening it courteously for her. But that meant she had to brush past him, and suddenly he was altogether too close, the cool clean scent of his skin overwhelmingly in her nostrils.

For a startled moment, her whole body seemed to breathe him, and she knew an overpowering longing to turn to him, to feel his arms close around her, to know once more the taste of him— the touch . . .

She felt as helpless as a puppet. Invisible strings were drawing her. Nameless desires were turning her limbs to water, slowing her instinctive flight. She wondered crazily what he would do if she put her lips against his skin, where the neck of his robe parted, and the breath choked in her throat as she realised exactly what she was inviting.

She couldn't look at him in case she saw in his face some recognition of her torment. Because if he knew—if he had the least idea, she would be shamed forever.

She thought, 'Oh, God, what am I doing here?' and fled, her heart hammering like that of a terrified bird.

CHAPTER THREE

SOPHIE never forgot her first view of Avirenze. It rose on the horizon in front of her like a clenched fist emerging from the silken sleeve on the sea, rocky and indomitable.

It was an arresting sight, and she wished that Mark was at her side to share it, but he'd spent the whole of the short voyage below in the luxurious saloon. To her disappointment, he'd proved to be a poor traveller. The turbulence they'd experienced on their flight to Naples had affected him badly, and he'd passed an uncomfortable night too.

He hadn't cared for the small *albergo* on the coast where they'd broken their journey. He'd said the bed was carved out of rock, and the pillow stuffed with concrete, and had hinted openly that Angelo Marchese might have found rather more glamorous accommodation for his guests.

Sophie, desperately embarrassed, had been forced to explain that the *albergo* had nothing to do with Angelo, but was the choice of her parents who always stayed there *en route* for Avirenze. Moreover she was sure that John and Barbara had overheard Mark's scathing comments, as he'd hardly bothered to lower his voice. Altogether, it hadn't been an auspicious start to the trip, she thought glumly.

She hadn't expected John and Barbara to be pleased that Mark was accompanying them, and she'd been fully justified. Not that there'd been any open arguments, or unpleasantness, she had to admit, but there'd been a tight-lipped coolness each time the situation was mentioned.

At the same time, they'd made it abundantly clear that their views of her engagement to Mark had not altered one iota, and the subject was taboo.

'Nothing is to be said by either of you,' John told her flatly. 'As far as anyone on Avirenze is concerned, you and this Mark are on terms of casual friendship only. I have informed him of this, and he has agreed. Now I want your word also.'

'Is this really necessary?' Sophie lifted her chin.

'Your mother and I feel that it is.' He was silent for a moment, then said gently. 'We are not really so hard-hearted, Sophie. You are still very young, and we wish you to have a breathing space in which to find out where your heart truly lies, without the pressure of promises and commitment which you might later regret.'

'I shan't regret anything,' Sophie vowed proudly. 'I love Mark, and we want to be married. You'll change your mind about him when you really get to know him. I know you will.'

John patted her hand. 'I hope so, *cara*. From the bottom of my heart, I hope so. All we want is your happiness, and when we are convinced that such happiness is centred only in this young man,

then we shall no longer stand in your way. You
have our word on this. Now, do we have yours?'

After a brief pause, she consented. After all, it
was only a minor stipulation, as Mark pointed out
to her next time they were together.

'It doesn't have to be official yet,' he urged
persuasively. 'Maybe it's just as well, as I
certainly can't afford to buy you the kind of ring
I want for you just yet.'

She shook her head. 'A ring isn't important.'

Nor was it, but the open commitment, she felt,
was. She was disappointed about her parents'
stand. She'd hoped for some miracle which
would reconcile them totally. Maybe, even make
it unnecessary for her to go to Avirenze at all,
because in spite of all the excitements of
shopping and preparing for the trip, she still felt
uneasy about it.

She hadn't seen Angelo since the night she'd
fled from his room. Thankfully, he'd already
departed by the time she got downstairs the next
morning, and she didn't have to face him in the
cold light of day. But, all the same, she was
unable to dismiss from her mind how she'd felt.
How, she reminded herself, he had made her feel.
Her reactions to him had shocked her, especially
as she didn't even have the excuse of alcohol to
blame.

And she was bitterly sure that he'd been
perfectly aware of her thoughts and emotions. He
was far too experienced not to have recognised
the need in her—the wanting that he'd so
effortlessly evoked, she thought with humiliation.

On Avirenze, she realised, she would be on his

own territory, very much in his power, and that disturbed her. Yet what did she really have to worry about when Mark was beside her?

And at that moment, like the answer to an unspoken prayer, he came to lean on the rail beside her, yawning and rubbing his eyes. He looked very pale, she thought with compassion, slipping her arm through his.

'Is that it?' He stared across the water. 'It's smaller than I thought. More mountainous too.'

'That mountain you're pointing out is a volcano,' Sophie told him demurely, and laughed at the shock in his face.

'It won't go into eruption while we're there? he asked apprehensively.

Sophie shook her head. 'It's been extinct for a long time. But the volcanic soil is what's made the island so fertile. My stepfather says the island has always grown much of its own food and wine. We can do some exploring perhaps—visit some of the vineyards.'

Mark shrugged. 'Maybe, but my time won't be entirely my own, you know Sophie.'

There was an odd note in his voice, and Sophie stared at him, uneasiness stirring again.

She said, 'Mark—don't hope for too much. The priority on this trip is to get to know my parents properly—to get them to like you.'

'Of course it is.' He sent her a smiling glance. 'Trust me, darling. I know what I'm doing.'

She thought, Oh, Mark, I only hope you do. Thought it but did not say it.

He went on, 'I must say that a couple of weeks in the lap of luxury won't come amiss.'

Sophie's tone was dry. 'According to my stepfather, Avirenze is where the Marchese family come to get away from that kind of thing. It's the simple life here—all oil lamps, and visits to the well.'

He said, 'You're joking,' but he looked horrified, not amused.

'Yes, I am, as a point of fact, but would it really matter so much?' She looked at him doubtfully, realising that—yes, it might matter after all.

She added colourlessly. 'Actually I'm sure there's no need to worry. We aren't staying at a *palazzo*, but I'm sure Angelo will have installed every modern convenience to help the simple life along a bit. After all, hewing wood, and drawing water is hardly his style.'

But even as she spoke, her mind was starkly invaded by the unwanted memory of the hard strength of his body, the uncompromising muscularity of the arms which had held her, and she knew she was not doing Angelo justice. He might work with his brain, instead of his muscles, but that did not make him in any way effete, she was forced to acknowledge.

Sophie bit her lip. That was not the kind of thing she needed to remember. It was an all too potent reminder of how perilously close she'd come to making a total fool of herself—not once, but twice. She almost gritted her teeth, remembering how insistently, how persuasively Mark had argued the case for approaching Angelo in the first place, overcoming her instinctive reservations, laughing indulgently as she tried to tell him that Angelo was too powerful, too dangerous, and that he frightened her.

I didn't know the half of it, she thought bitterly.

The harbour was tiny, rocky promontories closing it in on both sides like encircling arms.

She thought uneasily, '*Will you come into my parlour . . .*'

And it came as no surprise that the first person she saw, waiting for them on the quayside, should be Angelo himself. Not that she recognised him at once. The formal image was shattered. This Angelo, incredibly, wore ragged denim shorts, and a casual shirt open almost to the waist.

She watched him greet her parents, kissing her mother's hand and then her cheek, and felt a sudden flair of treacherous excitement as he turned to her.

But to her relief he made no attempt to touch her. He said merely, '*Ciaó*, Sophie. *Come sta?*' before turning away to give instructions about their luggage which was being brought ashore.

There were three cars waiting to transport them and their baggage to the Villa Giulia. Sophie found herself being ushered towards the second by a smiling young man who introduced himself as Fabrizio, Angelo's secretary. She made sure Mark was right behind her, yet when they reached the open-top vehicle, by some alchemy Mark was whisked into the front beside Fabrizio, and Sophie, to her acute discomfort, found herself sharing the back seat with Angelo.

It was absurd to feel so threatened, she told

herself angrily, trying to shrink not too obviously
back in her corner.

'I regret the cars are so small, Sophie.' Of
course he'd noticed. What did he ever overlook?
'But the roads on Avirenze are also—small.'

He was not exaggerating, Sophie realised as
they set off. The main street of the little port was
so narrow, they seemed in imminent danger of
sweeping passing pedestrians off the tiny pave-
ments as they edged along. Not that the
pedestrians seemed to recognise or resent their
danger, she had to admit. There were smiles and
waves all the way, rather like a royal procession,
climaxed by the moment when an unknown
woman, her face almost split in two by her broad
grin, tossed a bunch of white roses straight into
Sophie's lap.

'Oh.' Sophie lifted them to her face, revelling
in the gentle fragrance. 'How wonderful. Why
should she do that?'

'You must look like a bride, Sophie *mia*.'
There was a faint edge of mockery in the words
which stung, but nothing could spoil her
pleasure in the flowers. And it was an added
pleasure to know that her love for Mark and her
happiness were so evident that even a complete
stranger could recognise them.

The next lovely thing turned out to be the
villa itself. It sprawled on a rocky eminence
above the village, overlooking its own small
bay, a jumble of grey stone walls hung with a
riot of flowering vines, and roofed in faded
terracotta, drowsing in the noonday sun like
some great lizard.

'You like my home, Sophie?' Her instinctive gasp of pleasure had not been lost on him either.

'Oh, yes, although it's very different from anything I could have imagined.'

He smiled. 'What did you imagine, I wonder? Acres of white marble with an electrified fence and guard dogs?' He was smiling at her, and shyly she felt herself respond.

'Well—something like that, perhaps.'

'I have no enemies on Avirenze, Sophie. And no unwanted visitors either. The island has always been a sanctuary for our family since our earliest days, but I daresay John has already told you of this—and of *La Bella* Giulia for whom the villa is named?'

'No.' In spite of herself, she was intrigued. 'Who was she?'

'A beautiful girl, loved by an ancestor of mine. But because he was poor and she was an heiress, her family would not allow the marriage.' The amusement was back in his voice. Softly he added. 'History, you see, *mia cara*, has a habit of repeating itself.'

'I'm hardly an heiress,' Sophie said stonily. 'But let it pass. What happened to them?'

'They decided to elope. *La Bella* Giulia took two bags of gold from her father's treasure house as a dowry and left his *castello* to meet her lover. But—and here the story slips into the realms of myth—her way led through a deep forest, where robbers waited. They took the horse and the gold, and were about to rape her when, with a thunder of hooves, a unicorn came out of the forest and chased them away. Then, continuing its role as a protector of virgins, it carried her on its back to where her lover waited, and together they fled to Avirenze to hide from her family.' He paused. 'The house they built is supposed to have occupied the site of the present villa.'

'And did her family come after them?' Sophie asked.

He shook his head. 'Within a year, her father was dead—of an apoplexy, and her brother decided to forgive and forget. So, they returned to the mainland, and the dowry Giulia had brought with her went towards the founding of the Marchese bank.'

Sophie raised her brows. 'How convenient. I hope this devoted ancestor of yours didn't have that in mind when he proposed.'

'Why, Sophie.' The mockery was back in full force. 'And I hope it is not your own experience which has made you so cynical.' He glanced sideways taking in her rigid face, and her hands clenched tightly together in her lap, and grinned. 'But now you see,' he went on after a pause. 'Why the unicorn is included on our family crest, and is treated with such respect by us.'

'Yes,' she said. 'Because of a story the Brothers Grimm would have sneered at. Or are you trying to demonstrate that even high level banking has a human face after all.'

The dark eyes never left her face. 'Haven't you discovered yet, *carissima*, just how human I can be?'

She sent an almost desperate glance at the back of Mark's head, but he was oblivious, talking to Fabrizio, and anyway the noise of the engine would probably drown most of what Angelo was saying.

She said tautly, 'If you continue to talk like this, I shall leave—go back to England on the first available flight.'

'Perhaps,' he said. 'But will you persuade your would-be *fidanzato* to accompany you? Somehow, I doubt it.'

Sophie doubted it too, and the realisation did nothing to sweeten her temper, as the car swept under an arched gateway and stopped in a wide courtyard, with a fountain playing in its centre. As the sound of the engine died, doves flew up in a snowy eddy from a cote in the corner.

It was like being caught in some kind of timeslip, Sophie thought wonderingly as she gazed around her.

Beside her, Angelo's voice said softly, 'Welcome, Sophie. My home is yours.'

She managed a shaky, 'Thank you' before scrambling out of the car with more haste than elegance. Useless to tell herself that his words were simply an expression of a conventional civility. She knew that—but it hadn't prevented that involuntary chill of reaction, shivering over her, as if some promise—or some threat had been uttered.

Her first glimpse of her room helped to calm her. It was beautiful—the walls colour-washed in old rose, and all the drapes in white silk, minutely embroidered with tiny pink rosebuds. All the furniture in the room was antique, she realised, as was the old-fashioned canopied bed with its billowing curtains.

The fittings in the tiny bathroom which adjoined the room weren't modern either, but they worked with supreme efficiency. Sophie stripped and refreshed herself with a swift shower, then changed into a brief white skirt, with a matching top, coolly sleeveless and scoop-necked.

When she emerged from her room, it was to find Vittorio, Angelo's white-coated major-domo, waiting to escort her downstairs to the *salotto* for an *aperitivo* before lunch.

The *salotto* seemed to be full of people, and she hung back shyly in the doorway, searching the chattering groups for Mark, and realising with disappointment that he hadn't yet appeared. Then suddenly Angelo was at her side, his hand under her elbow almost inexorably, his calm, 'Come with me, Sophie, if you please. There is someone I wish you to meet,' stifling any protest she might have uttered.

People fell back, making room for them to pass, and Sophie saw they were heading for an elderly lady occupying a high-backed chair beside the imposing marble fireplace at one end of the room.

She was white haired and stately, immaculately garbed and coiffured, and Sophie aware of critical dark eyes surveying her, wished that she had chosen something more formal to wear.

Angelo said, 'Madrina, may I present *Signorina* Ralston who is visiting us here for the first time. Sophie, this is my beloved godmother, the Contessa Savaroni.'

Sophie uttered a shy, 'How do you do.' Her hand was taken and firmly pressed by thin fingers blazing with magnificent rings, and the Contessa inclined her head with a gracious smile. '*Felice di conoscerla*, Sophia.'

Sophie had the oddest impression she'd passed some kind of test, but she didn't have time to reflect on this, because Angelo was sweeping her onwards, and introductions were being performed on every side of her, or so it seemed. Her face ached with smiling, and she knew she would never, never remember any of the names, while her few words of Italian seemed to become more halting each time she spoke them. Not that it mattered, she thought, because everyone she met seemed to speak excellent English.

A maid appeared at her elbow, asking if she would like a drink, and she requested a Campari soda.

Angelo had been drawn into a conversation, and her parents were the centre of a laughing group on the other side of the room. At last she seemed to have a breathing space. Tall french windows stood invitingly open, offering an escape route to a broad terrace and the garden beyond, and Sophie took it, half-hoping that Mark might be there, as overwhelmed with introductions and new faces as she felt.

But the terrace was deserted, and with a little sigh, she moved across to the stone balustrade, and looked down at the gardens below, plunging steeply away in a mass of shrubs and vivid flowering plants, interspersed with the darker, more dramatic green of cypresses. She could

see in the distance the turquoise gleam of a
swimming pool, and even further away the
shimmer of the sea's deeper blue.

She leaned on the sunwarmed stone, drinking in
the scene before her. The air was heavy with the
scent of flowers, and busy with the hum of insects,
and Sophie lifted a languorous hand to move the
heavy fall of hair away from the nape of her neck.

She thought, It's so beautiful, and didn't realise
she had spoken the thought aloud until Angelo's
voice said drily, '*Grazie.*'

She spun round, flushing. 'You—you startled
me.'

'Then I must apologise. It was not intended.'
He held out a glass. 'I brought your drink.'

She took it with a brief word of thanks, feeling
absurdly tongue-tied yet again.

She said stiltedly, 'I was looking for Mark.'

'I expect he is still at the garden house,' Angelo
said. 'But the servants will ensure he finds his
way back to the house in time for lunch.'

'The garden house?' Sophie frowned a little. 'I
don't understand I'm afraid.'

He shrugged. 'It is perfectly simple. The
garden house is a small studio built by a great
uncle of mine who had pretensions to be an
artist. Mark will be using it during his stay here.'

She stared at him incredulously. When she
spoke, her voice shook a little. 'Let me get this
straight. You've dared—you've actually dared to
put the man I love in some kind of—shed in the
garden?'

'Don't be melodramatic, Sophie.' He sounded
almost bored. 'The garden house is extremely

comfortable, apart from its other advantages of course.'

'Which are?' she demanded furiously.

'Among others—removing temptation from your way. I told you, if you recall, that where my family is concerned, my standards of decorum are high.' He paused. 'When a couple are young, hot-blooded and in love, it seems foolish to subject them to the pressures of spending long summer nights under the same roof, when this can so easily be avoided.'

'You hypocritical swine.' Sophie was almost choking on her rage. 'How dare you insinuate— imply . . .'

'That you and your Mark would not sleep together if the opportunity presented itself?' He smiled slightly. 'It would hardly be natural to suggest anything else. And you, *cara* Sophie, are not lacking in natural responses as we both have cause to know.'

There was an electric silence. Sophie was burning up, with shame at his last jibe as well as anger. Suddenly the crowded *salotto* seemed like a refuge, and she attempted to move past him towards the french windows.

But Angelo's hand closed on her arm, detaining her. 'Looking for an escape yet again, Sophie?' he jeered softly, and she bit her lip savagely at this all too potent reminder of their last confrontation and the way she had fled from him. 'Because, if so, it is altogether too late.'

'It isn't too late at all,' she denied angrily. 'Mark would never have come here if he'd known you were going to—to insult him like this. We're free agents, and we don't have to stay here to be—manipulated by you.'

'Perhaps you had better consult with your *amante* first,' he advised coolly. 'Ask him if he feels insulted before taking any drastic action. His reply might surprise you.' He let this sink in for a moment, then added, 'He seemed quite satisfied with the accommodation offered to him.'

'But then,' she said between her teeth, 'You've managed to turn Mark into such an admirer of yours, he'd probably be satisfied with a bed in the coalhouse, if you offered it to him.'

'What a pity, therefore, that I have no coalhouse, and so we are unable to put your interesting theory to the test.' His voice was coolly indifferent. 'However, I still intend to ensure that you are adequately chaperoned while you remain in my house, and I am sorry if you had other plans.'

'I suppose I should be grateful to you.' Sophie gave a slight shrug. 'Especially if these—decorous arrangements of yours mean that I'm safe from you too.'

His mouth twisted. 'What a lurid little mind you have, *cara*. Will it reassure you if I promise I have not brought you here to seduce you? Besides, Madrina, who is my hostess here, belongs to a generation which believes in punctuality. She would hardly be amused if I kept her, and the rest of the household waiting for lunch, while I entertained myself with your delectable but untutored little body. So—you have nothing to fear,' he added with a casual shrug.

The fury inside her was rising to a scream, but with a superhuman effort she swallowed back the unladylike words forcing their way to her lips. He was baiting her, and to lose her temper would only make her more vulnerable than she already felt.

Instead, she tried to emulate his casual tone. 'Thanks for the reassurance, but it isn't really necessary.' She made herself look at him, coolly and directly. 'Because I'm not in the least worried. Oh, I'm not denying that you pack quite a punch, sexually, but then, so you should, because heaven knows you're very experienced. Yet that—initial overwhelming effect doesn't last, I'm afraid—or not for me anyway. It's all a little unreal—like this house.'

The expression on his face was unreadable, but she sensed anger in him, like a banked down fire.

'If that is what you think,' he said silkily. 'Then I shall have to do something to make it—real for you once again.'

She tried again to sidestep, to reach the french windows, and the approximation of safety they represented, but his arm was already round her, scooping her almost off her feet against the hardness of his body, crushing the breath from her, even before his mouth took a brutal, inexorable possession of hers.

She might have foolishly invited such a reprisal, she realised dazedly, but no imagining, no nightmare, no wildest dream could have conjured up such a kiss. She was terrified suddenly, the sun beating crazily against her closed lids, her hands thrusting ineffectually against the strong wall of his chest, and encountering with shock the warmth of his bare hair-roughened skin as she tried desperately to push him away.

All her bravado had vanished, and she was frightened—now that her rash words had incited the very reaction she should have moved heaven and earth to avoid.

Because there was no use in denying that this ruthless, forceful exploration of her mouth was inducing its own heated response in her body. A wild, shaking yearning was beginning to spread through every fibre of her being, and she was agonisingly aware that her small high breasts, her rounded thighs were beginning to ache exquisitely and wantonly for the touch of his hands.

She was blind, she was deaf to everything besides this sudden clamour of her flesh, forgetting where she was, or even the purpose which had brought her there—even ignoring the voice in her head which was insisting that this endless kiss—this intimate, arousing invasion of her mouth was wrong—wrong . . .

Only now—suddenly—there was another voice, and not in her head at all, Sophie realised.

A woman's voice edged with amusement, and something else besides, saying, 'So this is what you get up to when my back's turned, Angelo honey. Shame on you.'

Sophie felt Angelo tense slightly, and knew a swift shock of something perilously like disappointment as he took his lips from hers. She looked up at him uncomprehendingly, her senses still reeling from the passionate assault inflicted on them, as, gently but firmly, he put her away from him, his hands still gripping her shoulders, and she knew she should be grateful, because she wasn't at all sure her trembling legs would support her unaided, and it would be a double humiliation, if, after being caught in his arms by some perfect stranger, she were then to collapse in a heap on to the marble flags at his feet.

He said coolly, 'No shame at all, *cara*. Merely offering my little cousin from England a welcome to Avirenze.'

The newcomer gave a little laugh that was just too musical. 'If only we could all expect the same welcome.' She came forward. 'So you're Angelo's cousin. I'm sorry I wasn't around when you arrived, but Irving insisted on going all the way up to the crater this morning to take some photographs, and, of course, I had to go with him.'

She was young, Sophie saw, and incredibly beautiful with a mane of tawny gold hair rippling on to her perfectly tanned shoulders, displayed to their best advantage in a draped white silk jersey sheath. The dress was cinched to her small waist by a gold kid belt, and she wore matching sandals on her small bare feet. Her full mouth was curved in a smile which just missed out on genuine warmth as she surveyed Sophie.

Angelo said smoothly, 'Then you must permit me to introduce you now. Vanessa, may I present Miss Ralston. Sophie, this is Mrs Irving Carter.' His tone was faintly ironic.

Vanessa Carter's hand brushed Sophie's in greeting. 'So you really do exist,' she remarked. 'I must say we were beginning to wonder.' She laughed again. 'But now I've seen you, it's no great wonder that Angelo's been keeping you under wraps. Although he doesn't usually go in for cradle-snatching,' she added, with another head to toe assessment of Sophie which made her tingle with resentment.

She said very politely, 'I'm afraid I don't understand.'

Mrs Carter's eyes narrowed. 'Oh, come on, honey. You don't have to pretend with me. We're all old friends here, and we know what the score is. But you're going to find yourself up against some pretty strong competition,' she added with a little shrug. 'I guess you must be tougher than you look.'

Sophie felt as if she'd been kicked in the pit of her stomach. Her face was burning, and she didn't dare risk even a glance at Angelo.

He said, 'You are under a misapprehension, Vanessa *mia*. Sophie came here with her parents—for a little holiday, nothing more.'

Anger prompted Sophie to find her own voice. She said chokingly, 'And, as it happens, I'm engaged to be married, and my fiancé is here with me too. His name is Mark Langton,' she added, with a touch of desperation as Mrs Carter still looked sceptical.

'The engagement, until this moment, has been a strict secret, you understand,' Angelo said. His tone was smooth, but Sophie heard the undertone of anger.

'Well, I confess you surprise me.' Vanessa Carter threw back her head, rippling with well-orchestrated amusement. 'Oh, my poor Angelo. Actually beaten into second place for once by some British nonentity.' Her mouth pouted teasingly, and she put a hand on his arm. 'Does that mean you're open to offers, *mio caro*?' It was lightly said, but Sophie knew, with a sudden inward shiver of distaste that it was seriously meant. She stepped backwards, feeling foolish and intrusive, an unwarranted observer of a situation which embarrassed her.

She said hurriedly, 'If you'll excuse me . . .'

'Oh, don't run away, honey,' Vanessa Carter purred. 'We have an engagement to celebrate, after all. Angelo's just going to order the champagne.'

'Oh, please.' Sophie could feel the anger radiating from him almost tangibly. 'It—is supposed to be a secret . . .'

'Well, the secret's out now.' Vanessa Carter shrugged. 'And it's one great excuse for a party.' She gave Angelo another lingering smile. 'You're not going to be a sore loser, are you, honey. You'll drink to your—little English cousin's happiness?'

Before Sophie could forestall her, she had turned back into the *salotto*, her voice pitched to carry across the buzz of conversation and laughter.

'Irving—come and meet this sweet child. It seems we've been thinking all the wrong things. She's up to her ears in some secret engagement instead. Isn't that the cutest thing you've ever heard?'

Irving Carter detached himself from the group he was with, and came across to her. He was a big man, and years older than his wife, his hair already white, and a once-muscular body going to seed under the expensive sports clothes he was wearing.

'Well, Van.' The glance he gave her contained a measure of anxiety. 'I did warn you, honey, not to leap to any conclusions.' He gave Sophie an awkward smile. 'How do you do, little lady.'

Sophie murmured something in reply, acutely aware that everyone was staring at her. Vanessa's words had not been lost on a single pair of ears in the room, and she knew with a sinking feeling that the engagement she shouldn't have mentioned would probably be the talking point of the day.

She had caught a glimpse of her parents, and seen Barbara looking stricken, and John frankly annoyed. She bit her lip. She wanted to go over to them, and explain she hadn't deliberately let the cat out of the bag against their express wish, but had been provoked into it. But something held her back—something which reminded her that the provocation had stemmed from Vanessa finding her in Angelo's arms—and that was something she didn't want anyone else to know about, she thought, shame flicking along the rawness of her nerve endings.

'Sophie,' a voice said, and she turned with relief to face Mark. He was smiling perfunctorily, and there was an aggrieved expression in his eyes as he stared at her. 'What the hell are you playing at?' he demanded in a low voice. 'Are you deliberately trying to ruin my chances with your family almost before I get here? I thought we'd agreed to say nothing.'

'We did,' Sophie said wearily. She felt very close to tears suddenly. 'But there was this woman—a Mrs Carter—she began saying the most appalling things and——' she shrugged helplessly —'I suppose it just slipped out.'

'Oh, for heaven's sake.' He sounded thoroughly exasperated. 'I hope you weren't rude to her, Sophie. She only happens to be the wife of one of New York's leading financiers. My God,' he added, relish creeping into his tone. 'This place is like an informal gathering of the IMF. It's fantastic—the whole set-up.' He gave her a triumphant look. 'And you should see where I'm sleeping. It's palatial.'

'Some hut in the grounds?' Sophie took a little indrawn angry breath. 'I call it an insult. And I told Angelo so,' she added.

He looked aghast. 'You didn't. Are you out of your mind? Hell, Sophie, I know you didn't want to come here, but that's no reason to screw the whole thing up for me.'

'Is that what I'm doing?' she asked. She felt a little sob rising in her throat, and fought it fiercely. 'I'm sorry.'

It was his turn to shrug, ungraciously. 'Well, there's no use crying over spilt milk. But for goodness' sake watch your tongue from now on. You've no idea the influence some of these people have—the help they could be to me.'

She said stonily, 'Don't worry, Mark. I won't stand in the way of your rosy future. I'll even drink to it. They're bringing champagne right now.'

'Come over here, little lady. We're waiting to drink your health.' Irving Carter's voice boomed out. 'Isn't that right, Angelo?'

Sophie followed his gaze, and saw Angelo standing a few feet away, on his own.

In spite of the space between them, she was again breathlessly conscious of that same odd anger in him, reaching out to her, as if they were alone, entrapped in some private, bitter world.

It was hot in the *salotto*, but Sophie felt suddenly, icily cold. Angelo hadn't moved, but her hands lifted, as if to ward him off, because he was darkness, and the darkness was engulfing her, drawing her down greedily into unknown depths, and she heard her own voice, high and very young, saying, 'No' as she fell.

CHAPTER FOUR

'BUT I'm perfectly all right,' Sophie protested, not for the first time. 'There's nothing the matter with me—really.'

'Perhaps not, darling,' Barbara said soothingly. 'But you did have a very nasty knock on the head when you fell, and a few days rest can't do any harm at all. The doctor thought . . .'

'I know exactly what the doctor thought,' Sophie said flatly, a tinge of colour stealing into her face. 'And it wasn't anything to do with concussion.'

Barbara sighed. 'Well, it was understandable, Sophie. When a healthy girl of your age faints away, people are rather apt to leap to conclusions. Particularly,' she added, with a touch of grimness, 'When you've just forced your engagement to that young man down everyone's throats.' She paused. 'Has he been to see you today?'

Sophie shrugged evasively. 'Not yet.' Nor yesterday, if she was honest, she thought unhappily. Nor the day before that either. His attitude to her continued to be disgruntled, almost as if he suspected her of having engineered her faint for devious reasons of her own. There had been no point in trying to tell him about the chaos of emotion which had brought it about, so she'd passed on the doctor's diagnosis that she had been over-tired by the journey and adversely affected by the sudden change in climate.

'He says I must rest for at least four days, and keep out of the sun,' she'd told him, hoping that he would offer to stay with her and keep her company, but he hadn't done so.

He'd given her an almost perfunctory kiss, told her it was a pity she would be missing all the fun, and gone off to play tennis with Irving Carter.

From Fabrizio, who made a point of playing chess with her each night after dinner, Sophie had learned that Mark was spending the greater part of his time with the Carters, which she found depressing. When she rejoined the down-stairs party, she did not want to find herself spending her time in Vanessa Carter's exclusive company. But as Mark was clearly flattered by the attention they were paying him, she would have to proceed with caution.

She sighed inwardly. Another factor which had come to light was that the Carters were keen bridge players, and that Mark now made one at their nightly card parties, often, it seemed, held in the garden house.

Sophie had had to conceal a genuine sense of shock at the news. Mark had never mentioned a predilection for playing cards to her, but according to Fabrizio he was quite an expert.

'And in such company he needs to be,' he had added, capturing Sophie's bishop with an apologetic smile, on his way to yet another check. 'They play for very high stakes.'

She said lightly, 'Then I hope he wins' but inwardly her alarm was deepening. The comfortable dream of Mark developing a relationship of affection and trust with her parents seemed to be vanishing, and the fact that he was choosing instead to be with a crowd of high-flying bridge players seemed to have all kinds of inherent dangers.

It's all going wrong, she thought despairingly.

She said aloud to her mother, 'I feel so isolated shut away up here.'

'Oh, Sophie.' Her mother pulled a face. 'You've had a constant stream of visitors. The doctor's instructions that you should have a complete rest seem to have gone by the board.'

It was true. Everyone had been more than kind, and attentive to her. Nothing was too much trouble. Even the stately Contessa had startled Sophie by spending portions of each day at her bedside teaching her to embroider.

It was, she had announced, a womanly, serene occupation, eminently suitable for a young bride, and she had waved away Sophie's protests that as a working wife, she wouldn't have time for serenity. And she'd found to her surprise that drawing the coloured silks through the fabric was more enjoyable and releasing than she could have expected.

And to her even deeper surprise, had discovered that the Contessa could be more than approachable. She was not in fact resident at the villa, but had her own house further along the coast.

'But when my godson is here, he encourages me to visit him as often as I can.' She gave a little smile. 'Angelo knows how very lonely I became when my dear husband died. That is why he made me choose a summer home here on Avirenze, where I could be under his eye.'

'Oh?' Sophie had threaded her needle with some care. 'I didn't realise he was such a philanthropist.' She realised she had sounded unnecessarily waspish, and flushed. 'I mean . . .'

'I think I know what you mean, dear child.' The Contessa to her relief had sounded more amused than offended, and Sophie had been careful to avoid the subject of Angelo since. She had sometimes wondered what the Contessa would have said if she'd told her, 'It's thanks to your good, kind paragon of a godson that I'm stuck here in this room. I fainted because I was frightened—and it was Angelo who scared me.'

But she knew she never would. Perhaps it wasn't even true. Maybe, she had just imagined that violent wave of angry emotion, and her fainting fit had indeed been caused by the long journey and the sudden heat. She didn't know what to think anymore. And there was nothing in Angelo's cool courtesy when they met now to assuage her inner confusion. He was being the perfect host, she thought resentfully, wincing as she remembered her mother had told her that it was Angelo who had reached her first after her collapse, and who had carried her to her room.

Thank God I was unconscious, she thought vindictively.

When there was a light tap on the door, she looked up eagerly, hoping it might be Mark, but, disturbingly, it was Angelo who came into the room.

Barbara got up instantly, saying she must find

her husband, and Sophie put out a swift hand. 'Don't run away,' she urged. 'You've only just got here.'

'Nonsense, darling.' Barbara dropped a swift kiss on her hair. 'And I'm leaving you in excellent hands, after all.'

Sophie, bitterly aware of Angelo's sardonic glance, made no reply.

When they were alone, he said, 'How are you today?'

'Bored out of my skull,' Sophie said flatly, hitching at one of the pillows. 'Did you bribe the doctor to keep me cooped up here by any chance?'

He looked faintly amused. 'Now, Sophie, why should I do such a thing?'

'How should I know?' She sent him a mutinous look. 'Just part of your general programme for manipulating everyone you meet, I suppose. Although your scheme to bring Mark and my parents closer together seems to have gone astray,' she added crossly.

'Ah.' The dark eyes were hooded. 'The old adage, *mia cara*, of the horse and the water. I am persuaded you know it.' He shrugged. 'But after all, your Mark is an adult with the right to choose his own companions.'

She bit her lip. 'I suppose so, but why did it have to be those awful Carters.'

His smile deepened. 'You didn't care for *la bella* Vanessa? Well, why should you. She has few friends of her own sex.'

'But numerous men friends, no doubt,' Sophie could not resist retorting.

Angelo gave her a shrewd look. He said

smoothly, 'I never listen to ill-natured gossip, Sophie. Irving is an old friend, and has had connections with the Marchese bank for many years. I have always found his financial judgment sound, at least. Vanessa is the only major folly I can ever remember him committing.'

Sophie said, half to herself. 'He's old enough to be her father. What on earth do they have in common?'

He laughed aloud. 'Why, Irving has money, and she likes to spend it. Not an uncommon basis for such a marriage as theirs.'

'And that's all?' Sophie was horrified.

He shrugged cynically. 'What more do they need? And it is flattering for a man of Irving's age to have a young and beautiful wife, even if it means him spending hours a day jogging and exercising in an effort to recapture his own lost youth.'

'And they have bridge in common too,' Sophie recalled. She sent Angelo a hostile look. 'I understand Mark plays bridge with them too.'

He nodded. 'And backgammon with some more of my guests. He is quite a gamester, Sophie.'

Her brows drew together. 'Does he play backgammon for money too?' And when he nodded again, she said hotly, 'Well, can't you stop him? He can't afford to lose, as you very well know.'

'Perhaps he wins,' he said drily. 'Anyway, I think he would be justified in resenting any interference on my part in his pleasures. Besides, why should my persuasions succeed if yours have failed?'

Sophie's lips tightened. 'As a matter of fact, I haven't mentioned it to him yet.'

'Then I suggest you do so, if you are concerned.' He gave another slight shrug. 'But have a care. You cannot expect him to live in your pocket, Sophie.'

'I'm aware of that,' she said bitterly.

His brows lifted. 'Has he been neglecting you? Poor little one. Do you perhaps wish me to tackle him on that score too?'

'No, or course not,' she said hotly. 'And it isn't true. You're putting words into my mouth.'

'Was I?' He smiled faintly. 'I thought I was reading the look in your eyes.'

She flushed, avoiding his gaze. 'Well—you're wrong.'

'I am pleased to hear it,' he said mildly. 'Now is there anything I can provide to make you happier or more comfortable?'

'No, thank you,' she said shortly. 'I just want to be able to come downstairs and get on with life again. Can you persuade your doctor friend to lift his embargo? I'm beginning to feel like the Prisoner of Zenda.'

'I am sure Matteo will permit you to get up tomorrow. I will telephone him for an opinion.'

'Oh, that would be marvellous,' she said eagerly. 'Your godmother said that as soon as I recovered, she would ask me to have lunch at her house—with Mark, of course. She wants to get to know him. It's very kind of her, isn't it?'

'Madrina is a very kind person.' Angelo paused. 'And she likes you, Sophie. Shall I suggest the day after tomorrow as a convenient day for your lunch?'

She would have liked to have informed him she was quite capable of making her own arrangements, but that, she realised ruefully, would have sounded childish and petty, so instead she murmured, 'Thank you.'

He grinned as he got to his feet. 'Illness becomes you, Sophie. Do you know, you sounded almost demure?'

The door had closed behind him before Sophie could find anything to throw.

She lay back against her pillows feeling almost exhilarated. She was going downstairs tomorrow, and life was going to be wonderful. There would be no more coolness or misunderstanding between Mark and herself. She would make sure of that.

The last few days had been a temporary setback to her plans, that was all.

She thought perhaps Angelo would pass on to Mark that she was being allowed downstairs again, but there was again no word from him although she waited hopefully throughout the remainder of the day, and that evening.

And, what was worse, when she went downstairs the following day, he wasn't around. She'd wanted to say, 'Surprise' and run into his arms, and her disappointment was intense, taking the edge off the welcome she received from the rest of the houseparty. The Carters were missing too.

Fabrizio, who greeted Sophie with high exuberance, said that Mr Carter had gone out for his daily jog, in spite of the heat, and that his wife rarely got up before noon.

'But where's Mark?' Sophie looked around her rather helplessly.

Fabrizio hunched a shoulder. 'He is probably still at the garden house. He too is not an early riser, your *fidanzato*.'

'Then I'll go and roust him out,' Sophie said promptly. 'If you'll tell me where the garden house is.'

'There is no need for you to do that,' Fabrizio said slowly. 'I will send one of the servants with a message.'

Sophie sent him a glance compounded from amusement and irritation. 'I'm not an invalid, Fabrizio. I never was. Walking as far as the garden house isn't going to kill me.'

'Nevertheless,' Fabrizio looked embarrassed. 'It would be entirely better if a servant were to go. It is, I know, what *Signor* Marchese would prefer.'

Sophie digested this in a simmering silence. 'Do you mean—am I to infer—that the garden house is—out of bounds?' she asked at last, slowly and dangerously.

Fabrizio looked more ill at ease than ever. 'Not precisely,' he began.

'I'm relieved to hear it,' Sophie said, her eyes sparkling angrily. 'Not, you understand, that it would make the slightest difference. Dear Cousin Angelo's word may be law to the rest of the household, but it cuts no ice with me.'

Fabrizio groaned. 'Sophie, it is difficult for me when you say such things. Believe me, it would be better if a servant were to go . . .'

'And get heatstroke in my place?' Sophie raised her eyebrows. 'How feudal. I wouldn't hear of it.'

'It is what they are well-paid for.' His tone

became cajoling. 'Come for a swim with me, Sophie. You have not had the chance yet to try the pool, and when we've had our swim, Mark will be with us. You will see.'

Sophie shook her head, her mouth set stubbornly. 'Mark and I are engaged to be married,' she said coldly. 'If I want to be alone with him, I will, and Angelo can stick his double standards up his . . .'

'*Per Baccho.*' Fabrizio looked as if the next available fainting fit might be claimed by himself. 'You must not say these things,' he hissed at her, his genial face anxious. 'He is not always indulgent, as you find him here. Sometimes, when he becomes angry, he can be formidable.'

Sophie lifted a slim foot in a wisp of sandal. 'I'm shaking in my shoes,' she said sarcastically. 'If you're so worried about his reaction to my trip to the garden house, then don't tell him. And you needn't compromise your integrity by telling me where it is. The grounds can't be that vast. I'll find the bloody place under my own steam.'

She left Fabrizio looking glum, and marched down the terrace steps.

In spite of her brave words, the garden house took more finding than she thought. There were so many different paths to follow and so many of them seemed to double back on themselves to some focal point of interest like the tennis courts or the swimming pool.

But at last she came upon it, a small, low building set among a grove of cypresses. The door was shut, and the green shutters still closed across the windows. Sophie went down the slight incline which approached the entrance, and knocked at the door. There was no reply, and after a pause, she knocked again more loudly.

She heard Mark's voice sleepy and impatient. 'Come in. It isn't locked.'

She turned the massive wrought iron handle, and with a faint squeak the door opened on to a large room. In spite of the prevailing dimness, she could see it was comfortably, if not luxuriously furnished, with a fully equipped bar in one corner. The air smelt stale with alcohol and cigar fumes, and Sophie wrinkled her nose fastidiously as she took a step forward.

There was another door, half-open on the other side of the room, and Mark appeared in the doorway. He'd been taking a shower, it was clear, because he was wearing a towel draped round his hips, and drying his hair on another. His eyes widened incredulously as he saw her.

'Sophie? What the hell are you doing here?'

She had started to go to him, but the tone of his voice halted her. She looked at him uncertainly. 'Aren't you pleased to see me?'

'Of course I am.' He hung the damp towel over his shoulder. 'It was just such a surprise. I wasn't expecting to see you—and here of all places.'

She almost found herself saying tartly that it was no wonder he was surprised when he hadn't been near her for days, but she suppressed the hasty words. This was their reunion, their new beginning and nothing must be allowed to spoil it.

His arms closed round her, and she clung to him thankfully, offering him her mouth without reservation.

He said huskily, after a while, 'God, you feel—you taste fantastic. But all the same, darling, you shouldn't be here. Your cousin Angelo was quite specific about that. Besides, I thought you were supposed to be resting.'

'I've had enough resting to last me a lifetime.' She pressed her lips to his cheek. 'Surely, you knew I'd come to find you.' She smiled up at him. 'Let's have a look at your hideaway.' She moved away from him and began opening the shutters.

The sunlight revealed that it was indeed a beautiful room, in spite of the litter of dirty glasses and overflowing ashtrays still occupying the table, and the accompanying sprawl of cards and score sheets.

Mark saw her looking, and lifted a defensive shoulder. 'The servants tend not to disturb me in the mornings. I'm afraid it's a bit of a mess.'

That, Sophie thought, was an understatement, but she smiled at him. 'Mornings? It's nearly lunchtime.'

He groaned. 'Maybe, but I didn't get to bed till past three this morning.'

She picked up one of the score sheets. 'I didn't know you were a bridge fanatic.'

'I learned at school,' he said. 'One of the few social assets I acquired there. Don't you approve?'

There was a faint challenge in his voice, and Sophie bit her lip. She said quietly, 'I don't approve or disapprove. I just don't want you getting out of your depth.'

'Sophie the ever cautious,' he said derisively.

'Honestly, darling, aren't you a little young for this protective mother hen act? I'm a big boy now. I can look after myself.'

She winced slightly, turning away. 'I hope you can,' she said colourlessly.

'You'd better believe it.' There was a roughness in his tone. 'For heaven's sake, Sophie, you've been hostile to this visit ever since it was first mentioned. What's the matter with you?'

She said, 'I'm worried. I thought by coming here, it would make things easier, draw you closer to my family. But that isn't happening. I've hardly seen anything of you myself, and when we are together we seem to be at odds. I don't understand what's going on.'

'Nothing's going on, as you put it. You're imagining things,' he said impatiently. 'You surely don't want me tied to your wrist every minute of the day. And after you broadcast the news of our engagement like that, I thought it might be best to cool it for a while. After all, it didn't exactly make me flavour of the month.'

'I suppose not,' she acknowledged unhappily. 'But *you* didn't have to listen to Vanessa Carter, and her vile insinuations.'

He sighed. 'Oh God, you take everything so seriously. When you get to know Van better you'll realise she enjoys winding people up.'

She said hotly, 'Really? Well, I haven't the slightest wish to know her better, or at all for that matter.' Her voice broke. 'We're quarrelling again—and over what? Oh, Mark, what's happening to us.'

He came to her, sliding his arms round her and

drawing her against him. 'Don't sweetheart. It's all right.' He kissed her fiercely and for the first time, she had to force her response to him.

Mark muttered, 'We shouldn't fight. It's just that sometimes, it all seems so hopeless—your family's opposition—this half-relationship we have. It's so bloody frustrating.' He kissed her again, drawing her down beside him on to one of the deeply cushioned sofas. His voice sounded hoarse, 'Darling—I want you so much. If we belonged to each other, things would be different, I know it.'

His hands were exploring her almost feverishly, tugging her top from the waistband of her skirt to find the warm bare flesh beneath. He'd never touched her like that before—his fingers seeking and greedy, and Sophie felt herself flinching away.

'We said we'd wait—we agreed . . .' she began, but he interrupted her.

'Wait for what? For some future that may never happen? That may never be allowed to happen. I'm sick of waiting.'

He was pushing her back on to the cushions, his hand fumbling with her skirt, trying to force its way between her thighs. Her whole body was cringing, shivering away from his determination with something like revulsion.

She tried to tell herself that this was Mark whom she loved, but there was no conviction in the reminder. This selfish, aggressive intruder, his hand squeezing painfully at her breast, was a stranger, and an unwelcome one.

She said breathlessly, 'Mark—stop. You're hurting me.'

If he'd heard her, he gave no sign. His eyes looked almost glazed, and his breathing was harsh and hurried. His weight was heavy on her, restricting her own intake of air, and her movements. She was frightened, and becoming more so with every second which passed. She had visualised a wedding night, a sweet and happy coming together, not this—squalid struggle on someone else's couch.

She said, 'No' with force, and tried to push him off her.

'Yes.' The word seemed to be wrenched from him. 'Sophie—it's our only chance. Please—oh, God—let me . . .'

The approaching footsteps were like the answer to a prayer she didn't even know she had uttered. Mark did not seem to hear them, but the brief authoritative rap on the door had him sitting up, looking over his shoulder, swearing softly under his breath. Sophie wriggled free, her hands dragging at her clothing, trying to restore some order to them. It was one of the servants, she thought, come to tidy the house. She felt as if she'd been rescued.

Then the door swung open, and to her horror, she saw it was Angelo, framed there, dark against the sunlight.

He asked no questions. One long comprehensive look seemed to tell him all he needed to know. Sophie struggled to her feet, agonisingly aware of her dishevelled appearance, burning with embarrassment.

Every word seemed to have been sculpted from ice. 'Sophie—your mother is asking for you.'

'I'll come at once,' she stammered, shooting a sideways glance at Mark's flushed, sullen face. He muttered something unintelligible and swung away towards the bedroom.

Sophie walked ahead of Angelo into the sunshine, her heart hammering uncomfortably under her ribs, trying as unobtrusively as possible to tuck her top back under the waistband of her skirt.

He said, his voice dangerously soft, 'One moment, Sophie. Not so fast if you please.'

She cast him a mutinous glance over her shoulder. 'I thought Mother wanted me.'

'Naturally, she wished to know where you were,' he said. 'And she shared my concern when Fabrizio told us you had insisted on going to the garden house. I thought I had made my wishes on the subject clear to both you and your *fidanzato*.'

'I won't be dictated to like this.' Her voice shook. 'If I want to visit Mark, then I will, and there's nothing you can do about it.'

'I think you are wrong,' he said silkily. 'And if I can judge by the expression of your face just now, my intervention seemed overdue and more than welcome. In fact, you seemed to be finding the imminent loss of your virginity a less ecstatic experience than you had imagined.'

Embarrassment and fury warred within her. 'You're wrong ... we weren't ...' She stumbled to a halt at the cynical sideways glance he sent her. 'And anyway, it's none of your business,' she rallied.

'You have made this affair of yours my

business,' he said. 'And while you are under my roof, you will conduct it according to my wishes. Do you understand me?'

'Oh, I understand—only too well,' Sophie said recklessly. 'One rule for you, and one for everyone else. I'm expected to behave like some relic from the Victorian era, while you leap into bed with any willing lady who crosses your path. And talking of willing ladies—what about Vanessa Carter? Have you taken her up on her obliging offer yet? Of course, she's married to a friend of yours, but I can't believe either of you would let a little consideration like that stand in your way. After all—Gianetta Vanni isn't here, so you'll need some kind of consolation. You—hypocritical swine,' she added on a little gulp of rage.

'Why, Sophie,' he said too pleasantly. '*Grazie, mia cara,* for the keen interest you take in my more private comforts. But why this concern? A casual observer might well ask if you could even be—jealous.'

Colour stormed into her face. 'You egocentric bastard.' She lifted a hand and slapped him hard across the face.

There was a brief electric silence. Sophie's fingers tingled from the impact. She looked at the marks on his olive skin, and felt sick.

'The heat affects you badly, Sophie,' he said at last. 'I recommend a cooling off period.'

Before she could grasp what he meant to do, he had seized her, hoisting her over one shoulder as if she was a sack of potatoes. Enraged, she pounded at his back with her fists.

'Put me down,' she shrieked.

'In my own good time.' His voice was like molten steel. He was moving fast, covering the ground in long strides as if she was a featherweight, which Sophie knew wasn't true. She closed her eyes in revulsion as the ground whisked past, then opened them again to find that the gravelled path had given way to marble tiles.

He lifted her down from his shoulder, holding her easily in his arms. Turning her head, she saw the sparkling turquoise water of the swimming pool.

She said, on a horrified gasp, 'No—you wouldn't dare.'

'I dare,' he said softly. He walked towards the edge, holding her captive and helpless. The dark head swooped, and for a moment brief— endless—totally disturbing—she felt his mouth possess hers. His muscles tensed, and she was in the air, a welter of arms and legs and skirt, flailing downwards into the glittering blue water.

Choking and gasping, she surfaced, pushing her sopping hair out of her eyes, and swam to the side, hauling herself up the ladder, shivering at the clammy feel of her clothes. She was alone. Angelo had gone, and, thankfully, everyone else had gone up to the house for lunch, so her humiliation had gone unobserved.

She stood on the edge of the pool, and wrung the water out of her hair until she winced. The anger had subsided, and left shame in its place. She couldn't believe the things she'd said and done. She'd had provocation, yes, but not for the first time. And she couldn't deny it had been his cynical accusation that she might be jealous of his women which had sparked off her most violent response.

But why? It was a ridiculous insinuation, so why had she let it get to her?

It made no sense—no sense at all.

She stood in the sun, and shivered, wrapping her arms round her body. She needed to get out of these unpleasantly damp clothes, she told herself. That was all that was wrong.

Mark was her love. He filled her universe. So how could she even contemplate the possibility that Angelo's taunt about jealousy might have held an element of truth?

She said aloud, her voice shaking. 'It isn't true. It can't be.' And with more force—'I won't let it be true.'

Even to admit she was jealous of Angelo's women held implications which terrified her.

CHAPTER FIVE

SOPHIE looked at her watch, and sighed. She walked to the edge of the terrace and looked down into the gardens, but there was no sign of Mark. And Vittorio had already been to her to tell her the car was waiting to take them to the Contessa's villa.

Surely Mark wasn't going to make them late for their lunch appointment—particularly when it had been postponed twice already at his insistence.

Sophie bit her lip. Mark had been sour ever since his attempt to make love to her had been thwarted that day in the garden house, it had to be admitted, and although she could sympathise with him up to a point, his attitude was making it difficult.

Since that day, well over a week ago, their relationship seemed to have skated from bad to worse. The amount of time he chose to spend in her company was minimal. All her suggestions and invitations were immediately countered by his own plans. He was invariably swimming, or sailing or playing tennis, usually with the Carters. And although for the first couple of days, Sophie had determinedly made one of the party, if only from the sidelines, Vanessa's sly smiles and barbed remarks had soon driven her away. And when she'd tried a mild protest to Mark, he'd looked at her as if she was crazy, and muttered something unflattering about 'women's quarrels'. Sophie was left feeling that she was stupid and over-sensitive.

Perhaps she was, she thought, kicking irritably at a pebble. And perhaps it was just imagination that the other members of the houseparty were feeling sorry for her. Everyone was being just that bit too kind—too concerned to include her in their plans. By car, horseback or on foot, she'd explored nearly the whole island, gone water-skiing from the cove, and drunk far too much wine, along with everyone else, at a fiesta in the port.

But for Mark, she could have been enjoying herself one hundred per cent. And, but for Angelo . . . She avoided him as much as possible, and never voluntarily addressed a word to him, knowing all the time that he was aware of and amused by her covert hostility.

She had managed to get into the villa and up to her room unseen that day, and when she'd come down late for lunch, Barbara had exclaimed, 'Darling—your hair—it's damp.'

She'd said, lifting her chin, 'Yes, it was so warm, I couldn't resist going for a swim.' And met Angelo's ironic smile with defiance.

She would never forgive him for treating her like that, and so she would tell him, given the opportunity. Only the chance never arose. He obviously considered she'd been taught a sufficient lesson, because he made no attempt to seek her out.

Sophie had presumed he would apologise for throwing her in the pool, and had steeled herself to say she was sorry, in return, for slapping him, but for nothing else. It was frustrating not to be able to say anything at all.

And fuelling her resentment was the realisation that her reckless accusation about his relationship with Vanessa Carter had been perfectly accurate. Not that he neglected his other guests, Sophie grudgingly admitted. But the beautiful Vanessa was never far away from him, particularly in the evenings after dinner when concealed hi-fi units in the *salotto* played softly and there was dancing. And Vanessa danced exclusively with Angelo, her sinuous body held close in his arms, her eyes smiling blatantly with invitation into his. What Irving Carter thought about it, Sophie couldn't even surmise. Certainly, his beamingly compla-cent smile didn't bear a trace of jealousy or resentment.

Didn't he care? Or did he perhaps care too much, preferring to turn a deliberately blind eye to her behaviour rather than lose her? Sophie found herself shivering away from either alternative.

And she despised Angelo, she told herself, more than ever.

She heard footsteps and turned to see Vittorio approaching.

She said, 'I'm afraid *Signor* Langton hasn't arrived yet. Perhaps someone could go and see what's keeping him.'

'It has been done, *signorina*.' Vittorio spread his hands. '*Signor* Langton regrets he is unwell, and will be unable to accompany you to lunch with the Contessa. He urges that you enjoy yourself,' he added.

'Unwell?' Sophie echoed. 'But what's the matter with him.'

Vittorio shrugged. 'He thinks—too much sun, *signorina*. Unpleasant, but not serious.'

Sophie knew an overwhelming desire to burst into tears, but she controlled herself sternly. 'Then I'd better go,' she said stonily. 'I don't wish to keep the Contessa waiting.'

'No, *signorina*.' Vittorio agreed politely. 'I wish you a most pleasant lunch.'

'I'm sure it will be.' She sent him rather a taut smile. But her certainty was due to be short-lived, when she walked into the courtyard and found the car waiting with Angelo in the driving seat instead of the expected chauffeur.

She stopped dead. 'What are you doing here?'

'Madrina's invitation included me also.' Dark glasses hid the expression in his eyes. 'You have some objection?'

She had several, but it was useless to voice them. The Contessa was entitled, after all, to invite her godson to lunch if she wished.

She said, 'Perhaps you'd make my apologies. Mark—isn't well and I think I'd better stay here . . .'

'To nurse him?' Angelo asked derisively. 'Don't be a little fool, Sophie. Get in the car, and I'll take you for a civilised lunch with my godmother. You can hardly let her down again,' he added brusquely as she hesitated.

'No—it wasn't my fault . . .'

'I'm aware of that,' he said with thinly veiled impatience. 'Shall we go?'

She gave him a fulminating look, and slid into the passenger seat beside him.

It was only a short journey along a spectacular cliff road, with cultivated terraces rising in steps to high, bare rock on one side, and the sea, churning and sparkling on the other. Angelo made a few neutral remarks about the scenery and the weather which she responded to with brief and studied indifference.

It was unnerving to find herself alone with him again, and she wished desperately that Mark had kept out of the sun, and was here with her, bolstering her, protecting her . . . But from what? It was something she did not dare examine too closely, and that in itself was disturbing.

She suppressed a tiny sigh of relief when Angelo turned the car in through open wrought-iron gates, and negotiated a prettily flower-lined drive to the front of the house where the Contessa stood serenely smiling to welcome them.

She accepted Sophie's apologies for Mark with perfect graciousness, so much so that Sophie had the oddest suspicion that his non-appearance had not been entirely unexpected. Certainly the lunch table, set under an awning in a tiny walled patio at the rear of the house, was only laid for three.

'So,' the Contessa patted her hand. 'You yourself are well, my dear Sophie. And your embroidery? I hope you still persevere?'

'Yes.' Sophie grimaced comically. 'But I don't think it will ever be my strong point.'

The Contessa laughed. 'You should treat your work gently, Sophie. Pierce the fabric with your needle only, not—stab it as if it was your enemy.' She turned to Angelo. 'You would not believe how fierce she can be.'

Angelo's fingers brushed his tanned cheek as if chasing away some intrusive insect. He said coolly, 'I am already convinced, Madrina.'

Sophie glared at him, and accepted from his hand the glass of fruit juice she'd requested in place of an *aperitivo*. But by the time lunch was served, by a plump grey-haired woman, who was clearly a devoted family retainer, Sophie had begun imperceptibly to relax. The food helped. They had melon, followed by meltingly succulent fresh fish baked in the oven with herbs, and thin slices of veal in a sauce with cream and mushrooms, and a cold dry wine to help it all down. Sophie ate every mouthful, and the *zabaglione* which followed and sat back replete.

'That was wonderful.'

'Serafina likes to cook,' the Contessa agreed. 'It is boring for her having to cater for my poor appetite alone. Perhaps you will come again to see me, Sophie. I am selfish enough to enjoy young company.'

'I'd love to.' Sophie looked admiringly round the patio with its profusion of flowering tubs and hanging baskets. 'And bring Mark if I may?'

'Certainly,' the Contessa's voice was neutral. 'If he wishes to accompany you.'

But Sophie had seen the swift glance she sent Angelo, and rose to the defence.

'He would have been here today,' she protested. 'If he'd been well enough.'

'Of course,' the Contessa said soothingly. 'These indispositions are most distressing, but fortunately they soon pass. Now, shall we have coffee?'

And when it had been drunk, the Contessa announced that she wished to repose herself a little.

'Oh, perhaps we'd better be getting back.' Sophie half rose, but the Contessa shook her head.

'No, dear child. Angelo will take you for a walk—to see the grotto perhaps, and then Serafina is planning tea—an English tea in your honour with sandwiches and little cakes.'

With a smile and a little wave of her hand, she went back into the house, leaving Sophie uneasy and on the edge of her chair.

'Do you wish to walk,' Angelo looked at her, his brows raised interrogatively.

'No,' she said with more haste than civility. 'I—I think I'll just stay here. But don't feel obliged to stay. If you want to see this grotto . . .'

'I have already seen it, on more occasions than it is possible to remember,' he said rather drily. 'You seem anxious to be rid of me.'

Sophie bit her lip. 'Is it any wonder?'

He shrugged. 'Yet my intentions are honourable in the extreme,' he said. He looked at her half-smiling. 'Your instincts do not play you false, Sophie. Yes, Madrina has left us together deliberately.'

In a small, dry voice, she said, 'Why should she do that?'

He said coolly and quietly, 'So that I may ask you to marry me.'

She seemed to be enclosed in a silence made of sunlight, and the scent of the flowers, a silence which resolved itself into Angelo watching her, waiting, incredibly, for an answer.

She said huskily, 'Is this some joke?'

'I have rarely been more serious. Or did you think I intended to remain a bachelor all my life? If so, you are wrong. I have the same needs as any other man for a settled life, a home, children.'

His voice was totally unemotional. He might have been enumerating some of the Marchese bank's least important assets, she thought, staring at him.

She found her voice, 'And you think that I . . .? But you must be mad. You know quite well I'm engaged to Mark—that I'm going to marry him.'

'I am aware that was your original intention. It has occurred to me that perhaps you have had a chance to think again.'

She was taut and quivering. 'Is that why you invited us here—hoping that it would all go wrong—when you promised—you promised that . . .'

'That I would help you find your heart's desire. Is that how you still regard that mercenary young oaf back at the villa?'

'How dare you call him that?' she gasped chokingly.

'Why don't you face facts?' His tone was almost casual. 'Marriage needs a sounder basis than a first infatuation. Isn't that what you've felt for this Mark—and isn't it over?'

'No.' Her heart was thudding agonisingly. 'No, I love him, and if things have gone wrong, it's not his fault, or mine. It's this bloody island and the horrible people you invite here.' She stopped on a little sob. 'And it's an insult to think I'd ever ditch Mark just because we've had a few problems.'

'A proposal of marriage is hardly an insult, *mia cara*.' The cool voice had slowed to a drawl. 'And I am considered reasonably eligible.'

'Not by me,' Sophie said fiercely. 'I suppose you think I should be grateful. An offer of marriage from the almighty, the all-powerful Angelo Marchese. Was I supposed to be swept off my feet?'

He laughed. 'Not you, Sophie. I thought— perhaps—intrigued.'

'Not even that,' she denied angrily. 'Nauseated, maybe.'

He shrugged again. 'That is your privilege.'

She got to her feet. 'And now I'd like to go back to the villa. Perhaps you can explain to your godmother why I can't stay for tea.'

'She will be disappointed,' he said. 'For more than one reason.'

'I'm sorry.' She was trembling. 'But it's a preposterous idea!' She hesitated, not wanting to ask, but unable to resist. 'I mean—why me?'

'You are young, beautiful, healthy, and I think you could adapt to the demands of my world,' he said. He paused, then said with soft mockery, 'Or did you expect a declaration of undying passion, *mia cara*? I credited you with too much intelligence.'

'I have,' she said. 'And any talk of love from you would be ridiculous as well as disgusting.'

'You are nothing if not frank,' he said drily. 'Perhaps you would like to wait in the car while I make our excuses to Madrina.'

In the car, alone, the trembling increased. She sat, staring down at her hands, locked together until the knuckles turned white, and tried to come to terms with what had happened.

Angelo, she thought dazedly, had asked her to marry him. Wanted her as his wife. At least not—wanted in the usual sense. Had decided for cold-blooded reasons of his own that she would be—suitable. A home, he'd said, and children. Her fingers tightened round each other until she winced. Herself—her body—used and pregnant, while he continued to amuse himself as he thought fit.

Nausea rose in her throat and was rigidly controlled. She looked round restlessly, and saw the keys hanging in the ignition. It was the impulse of a moment to wriggle across into the driving seat and start the engine which purred into instant life. She released the handbrake and drove off. She had no idea whether the Contessa kept a car of her own on the island, and she didn't care. Let Angelo walk back to the villa.

Her hands gripped the wheel tightly, and she concentrated passionately on her driving, as the cliff road twisted and turned.

The first thing she would do when she got back to the villa was see Mark and tell him what had happened. Tell him everything Angelo had said. Surely then he would see that they would have to leave. And when they got back to England, she would forget about the secretarial course, and find whatever work was available, so that they could be married. And she would just have to trust to luck that her parents would relent about the Ralston legacy, once her marriage was a *fait accompli*.

She left the car in the garage area at the side of the house, and went straight through the gardens. She could hear splashing and laughter from the swimming pool, and voices and the rhythmic thud of shots from the tennis courts, but she saw no-one.

The garden house looked deserted, the windows shuttered like closed eyes against the afternoon sun. Sophie ran the last few yards and pushed open the door. The living room was empty. Mark must still be in bed, she thought remorsefully, he must really be feeling ill.

Perhaps he was asleep. If he was, she wouldn't waken him, but come back later and talk to him then.

But he wasn't asleep. And nor was his companion. One of the shutters had been left open, and the sun poured in, illuminating the bed like a spotlight, and the two bodies entwined there in the eternal rhythm of passion.

For a moment she stood there in total disbelief, her mind saying it had to be servants taking advantage of Mark's absence. Because for that same moment, she didn't recognise Mark in the stranger on the bed, eyes closed, naked body slicked with sweat, head thrown back, his face almost blank with pleasure. Oblivious of the fact that she, Sophie, was standing transfixed in the doorway. Recognition was beginning to dawn, not just for Mark, but for his partner, twisting and moaning beneath him, her tawny hair spread like a cloak over the pillow. Vanessa Carter.

She heard a sound rise in her throat, whirled round and fled, hearing the door slam behind her.

She began to run. She heard someone call her name, and gasped, tripping, grazing her knee on the path. If it was Mark, following, then she couldn't face him—couldn't bear it. Hands gripped her shoulders, and she fought them shuddering. 'Let go of me.'

Angelo said sternly, 'Sophie, be still. You will hurt yourself.'

For a moment she stared up at him, then with a little cry, she threw herself sideways on to the softness of the grass, retching miserably. When the spasm was over, he lifted her wiping her face.

He said, 'I took Madrina's car to come after you. I guessed you would go straight to the garden house—and what you would find. I wanted to prevent it.'

She shook her head. 'You knew?' she asked bewilderedly.

'Little happens in my house without my knowledge,' he said. 'And Vanessa,' he added laconically, 'had made it clear from the start that she was ripe for mischief. When I made it clear to her that I was not interested, she looked for someone else.' He paused. 'She can be very persuasive. Perhaps you should not blame your Mark too much.'

She said dully, 'I never want to see him again.'

'You claimed to love him. Aren't you going to give him a chance to explain?'

'What explanation is there?' Her eyes burned, her face very pale beneath the surface honey tan it had acquired. 'How could I ever trust him again—after this. I—just can't face him. I can't face anybody,' she added brokenly, the tears beginning to spill over. 'I want to crawl away somewhere and hide.'

'Then you shall.'

She felt herself lifted into his arms, and knew she should protest, but it was easier to turn her face into his shoulder and let the grief of Mark's betrayal have its way with her, her whole body shaking with sobs.

When at last self-control began to return, she discovered that they were indoors, and climbing stairs. But not the main staircase, she realised. This was part of the villa she had never seen before.

She said in a muffled voice, 'Where are you taking me?'

'To that hiding place you spoke of.' He paused, and opened a door, shouldering his way past it. Then he set her on her feet.

It was a large room, with tall arched windows looking out over the sea. Of the remaining walls, two were hung with tapestries, and the third gave access through a curtained archway to another room. There were Persian rugs on the floor, and two deeply cushioned sofas facing each other from either side of a massive fireplace. She saw a revolving antique bookcase beside one of the sofas, and nearby a table holding a chessboard inlaid with ebony and ivory with chessmen to match.

She said bewilderedly, 'What is this place?'

'My private suite. You can stay here as long as

you wish. No-one will disturb you.' He paused, looking at her. He said flatly, 'When you told me you never wished to see Mark again, did you mean it? Because it can be arranged, if that is truly what you want.'

'Yes—but,' she moistened her lips desperately with the tip of her tongue. 'Don't—hurt him.'

His mouth curled sardonically. 'I shall not harm a hair of his head,' he said coolly. 'I am a banker, Sophie, not some Mafia thug.' He paused again. 'I can also persuade Irving and his slut of a wife that they have outstayed their welcome. Is that also your wish?'

She nodded convulsively. She said, 'But wouldn't it be easier if I left instead? Everyone will know what has happened, and they'll be laughing at me—or pitying me.'

'And you are not sure which would be worse. *Poverina*. But it does not have to happen. Again, if you want, I can tell the rest of the party some story which will protect you from any speculation regarding Mark.'

'But people know already,' she said. She was remembering now odd comments which had been made to her over the past week, kindly hints, she thought, that she had totally misunderstood until this moment. People, Fabrizio among them, had been trying to warn her about what was going on. 'They know that Mark cared so little about me that he was having an *affaire* within days of my telling them all we were engaged.'

'It would have been simpler if you had kept the engagement secret, as John and your mother suggested,' he agreed drily. 'However, it occurs to me that there are circumstances under which Mark's behaviour could be understood, and even condoned.'

She shook her head wearily, 'I don't understand.'

'If Mark was seeking consolation because he had lost you to another man, perhaps?' The dark eyes held her compellingly. 'He would then be more pitied than blamed. And no-one would blame you for having overestimated your feelings for him.'

She began, 'But there is no other man . . .' then stopped. She said, '*You*? You mean . . .?'

'Why not?' He smiled faintly. 'You cannot have forgotten so soon that I asked you earlier to be my wife.' He shrugged. 'Once I tell your parents and my friends that I am engaged to you myself, then Mark's hasty departure will seem almost noble—an act of renunciation.'

'No-one would believe it,' she said.

'You think not? What if I told you that the news that we are to be married would come as a surprise to no-one? That many of my friends were stunned when you so rashly announced your engagement to Mark because they believed they had been invited here to meet my future wife, Madrina among them.'

Her legs wouldn't support her any more. She sank down on to the nearest sofa.

After a long silence, she said, 'But I did announce it. Nothing can change that. And no-one will credit that I—was in love with Mark last week, and with you—now.'

Angelo shrugged again. 'But if you'd made the

announcement through pique—because you were—mistakenly—jealous of Vanessa?' He smiled at her. 'You see, Sophie, explanations can be found. All I need is your agreement.'

Her skirt was dusty and torn, and there was a faint smear of blood on her leg where she'd fallen. She touched it almost absently her brows drawn together. She said quietly, 'Just what I am agreeing to? A story—or more than that?'

'I am asking you once more to be my wife.'

Still, she didn't look at him. She said, 'It's— quite impossible. Surely you must see that. Oh, I'm not denying you could get my parents to believe anything you wanted, and your friends too, but there couldn't be a—marriage. I loved Mark. Nothing can change that, and I have to get over it somehow. But not by—going to another man. It would be obscene.'

His mouth twisted slightly. 'Shall we reduce the problem to simpler terms?' he asked ironically. 'You do not wish to sleep with me.'

Bright spots of colour bloomed in her cheeks. She said, 'You must see that I—couldn't . . .'

'I am prepared to accept that,' he said almost casually. 'So—are there any other—insuperable barriers?'

Sophie gaped at him. 'You mean you'd be prepared to—not to . . . Oh, it's impossible. You told me yourself that you—you wanted children.'

'And I do,' he said calmly. 'But not immediately. If you wish to regard our marriage at first as a state of mutual convenience, then you may do so. I shall not force you to—outrage your finer feelings, *mia cara*,' he added drily.

She played with the rent in her skirt. 'Perhaps, but you're hardly one of nature's celibates.' There was a tartness in her voice which she instantly regretted.

'Ah,' he said softly. 'But I do not expect to remain celibate forever, Sophie. I prefer to take the view that at some future time—some day— some night you will come to me. At any rate the decision will be yours.'

'And you'll wait?' Her voice was sceptical. 'For how long, I wonder.'

'For a reasonable time,' he returned levelly. 'I make no other guarantees, Sophie.' He paused, grinning at her. 'Take a chance, *bella mia*,' he invited softly. 'Love has played you false, so why not marry for money instead. No-one will laugh at you for that.'

'No,' she said. 'But you're taking quite a risk yourself. What if I—never change my mind?'

He lifted a cynical shoulder. 'Never, *cara*, will be as long for you as it will for me.' He grinned at her. 'Believe me, Sophie, you are not one of nature's celibates either. Now—may I go down and tell them you have agreed to be my wife?'

'On my terms,' she said slowly. 'You may tell them whatever you want.'

'Of course. But I too have terms.' He walked through the curtained archway, returning almost at once with a square velvet covered box. 'I wish you to wear this for me.'

It was a ruby, dark as blood, and gleaming like fire in its antique gold setting.

'What is it?' she whispered.

'The Marchese ring,' he said. His hand closed

over hers, and she shivered. 'Wear it for me.' His voice was implacable. The ring slid home over her knuckle.

She looked down at it, her breathing quickening perceptibly. 'The badge of possession?' she asked bitterly.

The dark eyes were hooded as he looked down at her. 'I only possess what I am given, Sophie, and the gift is yours to bestow.' He lifted her hand as if to brush it with his lips, and at the last moment, turned it, pressing his mouth warmly and sensuously into her soft palm.

He said quietly, 'Through the archway you will find a bathroom, and a robe if you wish to shower. I will have one of the maids bring you a change of clothing. Dinner, I should warn you, will undoubtedly be something of a celebration.'

He smiled at her briefly, and went to the door. She watched it close behind him.

Sophie didn't move for a long time, simply sitting, staring in front of her, trying to make sense of what had happened. It was all like a dream, she thought dazedly, except for the giant ruby on her hand. That was only too real.

It was a commitment—but to what. To a marriage that was no marriage at all. To a man of whose attraction she was only too bitterly aware already.

The touch of his lips on her hand had pierced her body like a shaft of fire.

She touched the cool shape of the ruby with fingers that shook. The Marchese ring.

She got up and started towards the archway.

Action of some kind, even if it was only taking a bath, might stop this introspective brooding.

She was beside the table holding the chess-board, and she slowed looking down at it, seeing for the first time that the white knights had been carved in the shape of unicorns.

A unicorn, she thought. Where it had all begun ... And, holding the piece in her hand, she sank to her knees, and began to cry, not for Mark, but for the sweetest dream of her girlhood, now shattered forever.

CHAPTER SIX

SOPHIE adjusted the pearls in her ears, and smoothed one errant tendril of hair with judicious care. There was only one final detail, she thought. The Marchese ring which she picked up from the dressing table and slid on to her hand to join the plain gold band which now rested there.

Her face expressionless, she glanced round the room. It was large and, like the rest of the house, comfortably rather than luxuriously furnished. Not at all the kind of honeymoon destination she would have expected Angelo to choose, even though, when he'd asked if she had any particular preference, she had stipulated 'Somewhere quiet.'

Well, this was quiet enough, in all conscience. Isolated even, and perhaps she would have been wiser to opt for Paris rather than this rambling single storey house in the Bahamas.

'It belongs to friends of mine,' Angelo had told her. 'And promised to me years ago as a possible honeymoon retreat. It is reasonably secluded, but Nassau and the bright lights are within reach if my undiluted company should start to pall,' he'd added, the dark face faintly quizzical.

All the same, she'd been surprised to find the place so—homely, and about as far removed from the usual connotations of the bridal suite as it was possible to get. She'd been impressed too by the paintings which festooned the walls of the big living room, mostly local scenes and painted with flair in the same emphatic style.

'One of Anita's sidelines,' Angelo had commented casually as they looked around. 'Although only God knows where she finds the time with three children to look after.'

It would be a good place for children, Sophie thought, with the untidy, pretty garden sprawling down to a gently shelving beach.

'It's a lovely place,' she said, aiming for his own coolly relaxed attitude to the situation. 'I hope your friends didn't mind moving out for us.'

He laughed. 'Oh, Giorgio insists that we buy him the best dinner in Rome as recompense. They are looking forward to meeting you,' he added. 'Anita was desolated they could not attend the wedding, but one of the children had a virus.'

'Is Giorgio also in banking?'

'No, he runs a travel company,' he said. 'We were at school together.'

'Oh.' The unknown Giorgio and his painter wife didn't seem nearly as high-powered as the gathering on Avirenze, and Sophie felt almost relieved. But it drove home once more how little she really knew about the man she had married.

The wedding had been an ordeal for her, as had been the days which preceded it. She'd found the role of the radiant bride not an easy one to maintain under the circumstances, even though, to her amazement, Angelo had been quite right in his assurances that their patched together explanations would be believed.

When she had finally, shyly come downstairs,

she had been almost overwhelmed with the congratulations, and exaggerated compliments on her loveliness and Angelo's good fortune which showered on her from all sides. Mark and the Carters had left the island, how and when she didn't know and did not care to ask. And certainly no-one volunteered the information then or later. Their departure had not even seemed to leave a void.

It had been a shock to find that she was not even to be allowed a breathing space. She'd expected to go home to Bishops Wharton to make the preparations for the wedding, only to find that Angelo was arranging for the ceremony to take place in the little church on the island just as soon as the necessary formalities were completed.

'*Per Dio*,' her stepfather had laughed in jubilance. 'My cousin Angelo knows how to get what he wants. And he has been patient for long enough.'

'But there's no need for all this rush,' Sophie had protested with a sinking heart. 'He has no right . . '

'You think not?' John gave her a broad grin. 'Wait until you are married, little one. Angelo will soon teach you what rights he has.'

Which had done nothing to boost Sophie's fragile confidence.

Nor had the trip to Rome to acquire the obligatory trousseau. She'd protested to Barbara that she didn't need any new clothes. That those she'd bought for the original trip to Avirenze were largely unworn and perfectly adequate, but Barbara had just laughed.

Sophie had to understand that her new role as Mrs Angelo Marchese required a very different wardrobe.

'Oh, really?' Sophie had muttered. 'And where do you suggest we go for a wedding dress? Gianetta Vanni?'

'Sophie.' Barbara had given her an appalled look. 'I advise you strongly not to make any more cracks of that nature, especially in Angelo's hearing.'

'Oh.' Sophie hunched an irritable shoulder. 'Is his entire past a no-go area, or just *Signora* Vanni's part in it?'

'It's just no concern of yours,' Barbara insisted. 'Angelo may have—indulged himself during his bachelor days, but once you're married, all that will change. And it would be unfair—and unwise—to attempt to blame him for anything which happened before you became his wife.'

'I'll try and remember,' Sophie said with irony.

But she hadn't enjoyed the shopping trip. It was galling to know that every dress, every article of filmy, seductive lingerie was being chosen for its appeal to the man she was marrying rather than her own simpler tastes. Particularly when he wouldn't even be seeing any of the wisps of silk, lace and chiffon, the sultry nightgowns which embarrassed her even to look at them.

Everything designed with one object, she thought. To make her beautiful for Angelo.

But if he'd thought her beautiful when he turned and looked at her as she came down the aisle towards him on John's arm, her cloud of white silk organza billowing round her, then he hadn't shown it. In fact he'd shown very little at all, although grooms were supposed to be nervous too, just as much as their brides.

Perhaps to Angelo, the ceremony conducted by his uncle the Archbishop, who looked remote and rather stern until he smiled, had been just the conclusion of another satisfactory business deal. Maybe, to Angelo, taking a wife was little different to the acquisition of any other asset.

Yet, oddly, it had been almost a relief to find herself alone with him, and no longer the cynosure of all eyes, and any of her anxieties about his attitude to her once they were alone had been allayed by the casual friendliness of his behaviour.

Although she had to wonder what Simeon and Nina, who looked after the house and grounds, and also did the cooking, thought of a newly married couple eccentric enough to want another room to be prepared for them besides the master bedroom.

Sophie wished that the room Angelo was using did not, in fact, adjoin her own, but realised there was little she could legitimately complain about. She hadn't bargained for them having to share a bathroom either, she thought, biting her lip, but it seemed like quibbling to ask him to render her any further privacy. And the bathroom door was boltable from the inside, so she would have to be content with that.

She had spent the afternoon unpacking, then wandered through the garden, and down to the curve of silvery sand which edged the sea. There was a children's ball, lying under a flowering bush, obviously overlooked in departure, and Sophie suffered an odd pang as she looked at it.

What had Angelo said he wanted. A wife—a settled home—children? Well, she'd deprived him of all those at one stroke, and she couldn't feel any kind of triumph, just a strange, all-pervading numbness.

She couldn't imagine him as a family man, but she supposed he would want an heir—a son to succeed him. And in spite of his promise to leave her alone, there might come a time when he would question what right she had to deny him a child from her body. And when that time came, she wasn't sure what her answer would be.

She kicked the ball further under the bush, and into oblivion, and ran down to the water's edge, slipping off her sandals as she went. The house had its own small swimming pool, but it would be fantastic, she thought, to get up early and run through the garden to the sea to swim.

Well, there was nothing and no-one to prevent her doing just that, she thought, unable to repress the thought that in a normal honeymoon her husband might well have had plans of his own for the early mornings which would not have included swimming. She checked herself furiously. There was no future in that kind of thinking, although she supposed, it was inevitable.

After all, ninety per cent of the women at the wedding had been imagining how she would be spending her nights and envying her, she knew, and she couldn't blame them. Angelo's sexual attraction was so potent, it scared her, and the thought of spending this coming month virtually alone with him was more frightening still.

She glanced up and saw him coming down the beach towards her, and for one crazy moment, reality slid away, and she knew an overwhelming urge to run to him across the yielding sand and feel his arms close round her, and his mouth searching hers. And stayed exactly where she was, as if she'd been planted there, never to move again.

'Scowling, *mia cara*?' His brows lifted questioningly. 'Surely I can't have made you angry already?'

'It's just the brightness,' Sophie said feebly. 'I should have brought my sunglasses.'

'The sun will be setting soon,' he said, giving her a surprised look. 'That's what prompted me to come and find you. Nina is cooking us a special celebration meal, with flowers and candles, and I think she would like it if we dressed for dinner tonight at least. Do you mind very much?'

'Of course not,' Sophie denied, but in her heart she wasn't so sure. Nina, she thought dismally, was a romantic soul who realised that their wedding night, and the night which followed had been spent in transit. Separate rooms notwithstanding, she clearly intended to make it up to them.

Sophie had brought a selection of evening dresses with her, and in the end she had chosen one of the simplest, a silky black slip of a dress with narrow straps, its fluid lines accentuating her slenderness. She had twisted her hair up into a loose knot on top of her head, trying to hide her inner insecurity under a façade of sophistication.

As she got up to leave the room, she wondered if she had succeeded. Angelo made no comment though, his eyes drifting over her almost indifferently as he handed her a glass on her shy entrance to the living room.

'One of Simeon's special cocktails,' he told her. 'I guarantee one of the ingredients will be rum. But after that, it is anyone's guess.'

She sipped. 'It's delicious.'

'And probably lethal.' He sent her a brief smile. 'Do not say you were not warned.'

The meal was wonderful too. Nina served a mixture of local fruits in a piquant sauce to begin with, followed by baked Bahamian crab, and for dessert, a dark and ruinously rich chocolate mousse.

Simeon served coffee and brandy in the living room, then wished them goodnight and disappeared in a marked manner, leaving them alone together. He'd put the coffee tray on a low table in front of the big sofa, making it clear where he expected them to sit, and while Sophie had not ventured a protest in front of him, she felt uneasy now he'd taken his departure, and wished there was some unobtrusive way in which she could move.

They hadn't hurried over their meal, she thought, with a surreptitious glance at her watch. She could quite validly drink her coffee, plead fatigue, and retire to her room.

As if he had sensed her restiveness, Angelo said quietly, 'Don't run away yet, Sophie. I have another wedding present for you.'

'Another?' she asked dismayed. She already

had a sable coat, and a pair of exquisite diamond drop ear-rings, with a matching pendant on a delicately fragile chain.

Not to mention, she thought grimly, the Lamborghini waiting to be delivered to whichever of Angelo's various residences they returned to after the honeymoon. And when she'd tried to thank him, stammering something about his generosity, he'd given her a cynical look, and said, 'But isn't that exactly why you're marrying me, *mia bella*?'

Now, he took a small package from the pocket of his dinner jacket, and handed it to her. More jewellery, was her first thought, but as she began to unfasten the wrappings, and felt the shape within, then she knew.

'My unicorn,' she exclaimed in delight. 'You've given it back to me. Oh, that's wonderful. I've really missed it,' she added with a little sigh of pleasure, putting the tiny glass figure gently down on the table.

'Does its bargaining power work both ways, Sophie?' he asked. His voice was level, but there was a note in it which sent a frisson of alarm running through her. She looked at him. He had turned to watch her, and he suddenly seemed much closer, the long, muscular thigh only inches from her own.

'I don't know what you mean.' Even to her own ears, her voice sounded breathless.

'Don't you?' He smiled slightly, then put out a hand, and almost casually began to remove the pins one by one from her hair, letting the soft blonde strands cascade through his fingers. She sat rigid and motionless, unable to voice any kind of protest while her heart began to thud slowly and unevenly. 'Yet it is quite simple. The understanding between us was that the unicorn was a pledge—which could be redeemed at any time—for a favour. You asked one of me, even though it may not have turned out as you expected. And now it is my turn to ask a favour of you.'

She didn't need to ask what it was. It was there—in the naked hunger in his eyes as he looked at her. In his hand, gently sliding down the strap of her dress to bare her shoulder for his lips.

As his mouth touched her skin, her whole body shivered, but with anticipation, not fear. He kissed her softly, holding her in one arm, tipping her head back against his shoulder so that his lips could explore her throat, and the smooth curve at its base, where the pulse was going frantic.

His hand stroked her cheek, his finger moving down to trace the soft outline of her lips, already parted in mute invitation to his kiss. Everywhere he touched her was sensation, small separate coils of response, blending, coming together to form a bewildering, burning need.

His head lifted fractionally, and he began to kiss her face, his lips moving slowly and tantalisingly along her hairline, across her half-closed eyelids, down her flushed cheeks, to hover softly and sensuously at the corners of her mouth. His caresses were feather-light, beguiling, a silken thread leading her into a subtle maze of pleasure.

Without haste, he slipped down the other strap

of her dress, his fingers lingering, tracing the delicacy of the bone structure under the soft skin. His hand moved, and she felt the zip of her dress glide downwards, the brush of the silky material as it fell away, baring her to the waist.

He looked down at her, the tenor of his breathing changing to a sudden harshness, a new, fierce purpose in his face. He gathered her up towards him, the immaculate frills of his evening shirt grazing the taut peaks of her naked breasts in delicious abrasive torment, and his mouth possessed hers in an aching, passionate invasion, which drained her sweetness, and left her breathless, yet burning for more.

He lifted his head slowly, his hand stroking down the length of the slender body, arched in compliance over his supporting arm, to find her loosened dress and ease it down over her hips.

Sophie lifted weighted eyelids and looked up at him, and a little sound rose in her throat. Suddenly his face had become a stranger's—the face of her master, she thought hysterically, enjoying his latest and easiest conquest.

Her hands had been lifting, almost of their own volition, to cradle his head, to draw him down to her again, but now they were against his chest, tangling in the crisp linen shirt, pushing at him in panic.

She said hoarsely, 'Let me go. Don't touch me. You—you promised . . .'

He was very still, his whole body taut. Under her palms, his heart was racing.

He said, 'Sophie don't be a little fool. You want this as much as I do.'

'No—no, I don't.' Her head thrashed almost wildly from side to side in negation—in rejection. 'Oh God, I should have known I couldn't trust you—you swine . . .'

For a long moment he was silent, his face set starkly, his mouth tight and compressed. Then he sat up, lifting one shoulder in a shrug that was almost negligent.

'Calm yourself,' he advised her coolly. 'No lasting damage has been done to your chastity.'

He lifted her upright briskly, pulling up her dress to cover her, closing the zip with casual expertise.

'Is that sufficient reassurance?' he asked almost contemptuously.

Colour flooded her face. She couldn't look at him. She knew she hadn't been far from the point of no return when she'd panicked, and realised he must know that too. And in spite of her protests, he must now think she was a pushover, like any of his other women. A little sob rose in her throat and was stifled.

He sighed, a sound compounded of weariness and exasperation. 'Go to bed, Sophie,' he commanded brusquely. 'I regret that you will find no lock on the door—Anita and Giorgio would find such a thing incomprehensible—so you will just have to take my word that you have nothing else to fear from me, tonight or any other night,' he added bitingly.

She had reached the door, when he said abruptly, 'Wait.'

She paused, glancing back apprehensively at him over her shoulder. He came across to her and put the little glass unicorn in her hand, closing her fingers round it. 'It is still yours,' he said. The dark eyes rested on her mouth for a moment, and he gave a brief crooked smile. 'And if you ever change your mind,' he told her softly. 'Then you need do no more than return it to me.'

He turned away from her, strolling back to the sofa, and pouring himself another brandy.

Safe in her room, Sophie unclenched her hand and looked numbly at the glass unicorn. She should have thrown it at him, she thought in outrage. She should have dropped it on the floor, and ground it into powder with her heel.

Yet, she hadn't done so, and presently, she put it gently on the table beside the bed, and lay, watching it, until eventually, against all the odds, she drifted into sleep.

By the end of the second week, Sophie realised that Angelo had told her no more than the truth. He'd made no further approaches to her of any kind, either by word, look, or gesture. Nor did he make any particular effort to seek her company, and except at mealtimes, she saw little of him.

To her surprise, she realised he was spending part of every day working, with telephone calls taking up most of the time. Letters and documents seemed to arrive for him by every post, and she could sense Simeon and Nina's total bewilderment with the situation, although they were too discreet to let it become overt.

When they did meet, he was friendly enough, if impersonal, making some brief, polite comment about the weather, or her well-being and at times, she thought crazily, it seemed the lover who had kissed and caressed her with such devastating sensual tenderness must have been a figment of her imagination. But the glitter of the little unicorn beside her bed was a potent reminder that she had imagined nothing.

The glass figure was no longer a talisman, she thought wryly, but more of a sexual timebomb. Although she could never, even in her wildest dreams, imagine herself going to him, and meekly handing over the unicorn as a sign of submission.

Even though she might want to. For, as each day passed, the awful truth was she was becoming more and more aware of him in a way she had never imagined possible.

Safely concealed behind her sunglasses, she watched him hungrily whenever she had the opportunity, absorbing every little detail almost obsessively as she had never allowed herself to do previously.

She had never realised until then the sheer instinctive grace of his lean, powerful body, whether he was walking or swimming, or simply lounging in the sun. She watched the incisive way he moved his hands when he was talking, the cold purity of his profile, nose and chin strongly and arrogantly marked, the way the black silky hair grew to a peak on his forehead.

Living in such close proximity to him, she noticed his fastidiousness too in every way. He accepted food and drink as some of life's pleasures, but didn't indulge in either of them to excess.

It was as if she was learning him by heart, from

the shape of his mouth to the flare of every muscle under the smooth bronze skin, and the small black mole on his right shoulder blade, and she was bewildered by her own intensity.

How could she feel like she did, when only a matter of weeks before she had been in love with Mark, planning to marry him? If it hadn't been for Mark's betrayal, she would not even be here. That was what she needed to remember. She should be grieving over that, trying to work out what had gone wrong between them, not brooding over Angelo, who had only married her because she was young and healthy and had had the right kind of up-bringing. Yet, if she was honest, she found that altogether more galling than anything Mark had done.

She turned restlessly on to her stomach, and saw her husband approaching down the beach. He was carrying a towel and a magazine, and wearing the brief trunks that Sophie had already realised were a concession to their strange relationship. If the honeymoon had been conducted along usual lines, on this secluded and totally private little beach, with no danger of being overlooked from the house, she guessed he would have worn nothing, and persuaded her to do the same.

As he passed her, he said pleasantly, 'You need some more lotion, Sophie, or you are going to burn.'

He did not, she noted crossly, as she reached for the bottle and uncapped it, offer to apply the lotion himself. When she had finished, she put the bottle back in her bag with a little sigh.

He glanced at her. 'You are bored? Perhaps it would have been better to go somewhere more entertaining. I am sorry.'

'No, it's lovely here,' Sophie said swiftly, sitting up, and resisting the urge to tug decorously at the brief cups of her bikini bra. 'Very tranquil.'

'Perhaps too tranquil,' Angelo said drily. 'Would you like to have dinner in Nassau tonight, and perhaps go to a nightclub afterwards?'

'It—sounds very nice,' she said politely. Then smiled a little. 'And it will give me another chance to dress up.'

It wasn't until she saw the enigmatic glance he gave her before returning his attention to the magazine, that she remembered the last occasion she had dressed for dinner—only to end up almost naked in his arms. It was obvious he hadn't forgotten at all, and she only hoped he didn't think her reference had been intentionally provocative.

But at least for this one evening, they wouldn't be on their own, she offered herself as a palliative. Tonight she could take refuge behind other people.

She dressed with care when the time came, bearing in mind it was her first real appearance in public as Angelo's wife, and wanting to do him credit.

The dress she chose was one of her prettiest, white threaded with silver, with a full and floating skirt, and a deeply slashed bodice, hinting to the point of indiscretion at the soft contours of her breasts. She wore Angelo's diamonds in her ears and at her throat, and just for fun, added the faintest frosting of glitter on her cheekbones and in her cleavage.

Simeon had brought the car round to the door, a sports model of an earlier vintage than Angelo would normally be used to. He grimaced slightly as he turned the key in the ignition, murmuring, '*Ecco*, a miracle' when it started first time.

The restaurant he had chosen turned out to be a hilltop mansion built in the early nineteenth century.

A watchful commissionaire leaped forward to park the car for them, and they were shown into a vast bar, furnished overwhelmingly in crimson velvet with a striped flock wallpaper.

They were walking to a vacant table when a loud jovial voice exclaimed, 'Angelo Marchese. Well, I'll be a son of a gun.'

Sophie saw the flicker of annoyance tighten Angelo's lips, but he was smiling civilly by the time he turned.

'Thompson,' he commented. 'And Lydia too. How charming. I did not expect to see you here.'

'Nor we you—although we saw the news about your marriage in the papers. And this must be the lucky little lady,' he added, bestowing a crushing handshake on Sophie. He was big and bluff with prematurely white hair, and his wife was fighting her middle years with ferocious chic.

'My dear,' she greeted Sophie. 'We really don't mean to butt in on your honeymoon. In fact we're only in Nassau for a couple of days. We've been cruising on Lloyd and Tish's yacht,' she

went on, indicating the couple they were with.
'Isn't it just an amazing coincidence that we
should all run into each other like this.'

'Amazing,' Sophie agreed.

Thompson Brand was taking charge. 'Now you
lovely people will have dinner with us,' he said
firmly. 'You're an old married man now Angelo.
You can't keep your lovely bride exclusively to
yourself forever, you know,' he added with a
chuckle.

Tish Curzon, a thin woman with a sour look
about her mouth, intervened. 'Oh, for heaven's
sake Thompson. I expect the poor girl is quite
glad of a break from all that everlasting
togetherness. Honeymoons can be very over-
rated pastimes,' she added with a shrug. 'Even
when you've managed to land the most attractive
man in the Western Hemisphere it doesn't make
that endless view of the bedroom ceiling any less
tedious.'

Sophie felt helpless colour rise in her face.
There'd been a salacious note in the other
woman's voice, and a look in her pale eyes which
she found utterly repellent. But, she supposed
resignedly, this was the sort of speculation she
would have to accustom herself to.

Barbara's lessons in company manners were
going to stand her in good stead, she decided
grimly, setting herself to endure Lydia's gushing,
and parry Tish Curzon's questions with gentle
dignity.

It was easier when the menus arrived,
Thompson Brand advising Sophie to have the
speciality of the house which was grouper,

cooked with mushrooms, sweet peppers and herbs.

'Although the conch creole is superb here too,' Lydia added graciously.

'And after dinner we thought we'd go on to the Boathouse Club,' Thompson went on. 'They have this fantastic female vocalist there. You can't come to Nassau and miss her.'

Sophie who'd been hoping to stage a diplomatic retreat after coffee had been served, smothered a groan. She stole a look at Angelo under her lashes to see how he was taking all this, but he was talking to Lloyd Curzon, his expression one of courteous interest.

She was unable to fault the meal, however, which they ate outside on a candle lit terrace. The sky was thick with stars, and the faintest of breezes stirred the blossoms on the trellised screen which gave their table privacy.

It was one of the most romantic settings Sophie had ever encountered, and suddenly she realised that other people were not a necessary barrier for her to take refuge behind, but bitterly irksome. If she and Angelo could have dined alone, she thought with a little inward sigh, perhaps there might have been some kind of *rapprochement*. Maybe even a miracle . . .

'Try the guava cheesecake,' urged Mrs Brand. 'Unless you'd prefer the iced soufflé.'

While they were waiting for their cars to be brought round for the drive to the Boathouse Club, Sophie managed to get her first private word with her husband.

'Do we have to go?' she whispered.

He shrugged indifferently. 'Accepting dull invitations is part of life,' he told her coolly. 'And this fits in with our own plans. Smile, *cara*,' he added carelessly. 'We don't have to see them again after tonight.'

The Boathouse Club was dark and intimate and very crowded, but by some magic a table was found for them right on the edge of the dance floor. Lloyd Curzon who'd been drinking his way steadily through dinner, and who was becoming flushed and a little raucous, Sophie noticed with faint distaste, ordered a round of Club Specials— an intriguing blend of fruit flavours with the strong kick of rum not too far below the surface. After a cautious sip, Sophie decided hers had better last her the rest of the evening.

The band, a small jazz combo, was excellent, she had to admit, and the singer, Nicole, when she appeared turned out to be a spectacular Creole in a silver lamé dress which clung like a second skin, leaving nothing to the imagination. She had a warm sultry voice, and the lyrics she chose suited it well, dealing with love in all its aspects in a way which veered from the tender to the risque, and on to the frankly ribald. It was a sophisticated, sexy act, and the audience were loving it, going up in flames, especially when Nicole began to move between the tables, picking out individual male customers and aiming seductively murmured verses at them.

Sophie supposed it was inevitable that she should come to their table. Thompson and Lloyd Curzon received only token attention, however. It was Angelo who got the full treatment,

Nicole's eyes widening in frankly sensuous appreciation as she looked at him.

Nor did she only look. Draping herself across the arm of his chair, she let her fingers trail down his arm, and brush his face and hair, while she sang to him, her lowered voice and intimate smile conveying to everyone in the room that this song was for him, and him alone.

It was quite a performance, Sophie thought, taut with outrage, and she wondered why Nicole didn't climb into Angelo's lap and have done with it.

He, of course, wasn't outraged at all, or even faintly embarrassed. He was smiling back at Nicole with equal appreciation, looking straight into her eyes as she drawled every provocative word to him. And when the song ended, amid thunderous applause, and she leaned forward to kiss him on the lips, he met her more than halfway.

She got up in one sinuous movement, bowed to the rest of the room, and vanished.

'Now follow that,' Tish Curzon suggested to no-one in particular.

Sophie discovered she was gripping her glass far too tightly, and released it with a certain amount of care. She was shaking inside suddenly, little flames of temper curling along her veins.

'Come and dance.' Lloyd Curzon took her hand, pulling her out of her chair. 'We'll show these people a thing or two.'

Sophie found herself propelled on to the dance floor before she could protest. She hadn't the slightest wish to dance with Lloyd who was even less sober than he'd been when they arrived. His hands felt clammy, and he held her much too tightly, and she couldn't back away without making some kind of scene.

'You're a real beauty, do you know that,' he said after a while. 'But you aren't Angelo's usual style at all. He likes them worldly wise as a rule, not out of the cradle.' He leered at her, his breath heavy with alcohol. 'Starting from square one with a lady must be a novelty for him.'

She didn't answer, her body rigid with disgust.

'You don't talk much, do you?' he complained. 'But come to that, you don't look very married either. So what does he do?' he went on, lowering his voice suggestively. 'Leave the marks in places they don't show?'

Sophie wrenched herself free, and ignoring his plaintive, 'Hey—what did I do?' went back to the table, just in time to see a waiter handing Angelo a slip of paper, and Angelo tucking it into the breast pocket of his dinner jacket. It could have been the bill, but Sophie knew it wasn't. The waiter's whole attitude was amused, conspiratorial.

Sophie sank down on to her chair, ignoring the vicious look Tish Curzon sent her as her husband came stumbling back to the table alone. She knew what that slip of paper was—it was a message from Nicole, and the knowledge pierced her like a knifeblade. He'd told her himself that he would wait a reasonable time for her, but would make no other guarantees. Those had been his exact words, and she knew now how to interpret them. He'd meant that if she was not available to him, he would find someone who was. And tonight a suitable candidate had fallen into his arms. Literally.

Her nails dug wincingly into the palms of her hands. She looked across at Angelo, and pitching her voice so that there could be no mis-understanding, she said, 'I'm rather tired. I would like to go home.'

There was a flurry of half-hearted protests from the others, and then the usual round of good nights.

And what a meaningless phrase 'Good night' was, Sophie thought bitterly. Here she was saying it over and over again, and she was having one of the worst evenings of her life.

Outside the club, she took long gulps of air into her shuddering lungs.

Angelo was staring at her frowning. 'What is it, Sophie. Are you ill?'

'No, not ill,' she returned off the top of her voice. 'Just tired. I'm allowed to be tired, aren't I?'

He shrugged. 'You are allowed to be anything you please—except bad-tempered—or uncivil,' he added rather grimly. 'You may not have cared for our hosts, but you could have made your departure a little less abrupt.'

'I'll bear that in mind for next time. There will be a next time, I presume. I'm sure if we look there'll be all kinds of delightful people stopping off in Nassau that we can spend the evening with. I can practise being nice.'

'It could take some practice,' he said coldly. 'I

am sorry the evening turned out as it did, but it was unavoidable.'

'I know,' she said. 'They're clients of the bank. And that man Curzon is revolting.'

'Why?' he asked crushingly. 'Wouldn't he take his hands off you when you told him to? How distressing for you, my little virgin.'

She said between her teeth, 'Perhaps you should have warned me that being mauled was all part of the job. No doubt, you find it a pleasure, as witness tonight's little performance.'

'Why, Sophie.' There was a note of unholy amusement in his voice. 'Is it possible you did not enjoy the cabaret?'

Sophie bit her lip, annoyed with herself. 'That's not important,' she snapped. 'But for future reference, I'd rather not be in the company of drunks who ask crude and insulting questions.'

'Poor Lloyd. What can he have said to provoke such a reaction?' He was silent for a moment. 'Let me guess. He wished to know why, in the middle of your honeymoon, you are still totally untouched? Am I right?'

'He's vile,' was all Sophie would admit to.

'But shrewd you must agree,' Angelo said cuttingly. 'His speculation may be ill-mannered, but it is understandable. Perhaps he felt that if I had failed you as a lover, he might offer himself as a substitute.'

'While you entertain yourself with that—witch, Nicole.' The words were out before she could prevent them, and she heard them and their implications with a kind of horror.

'Beware, Sophie,' he said after a pause. 'You are beginning to sound like a jealous wife. And yet, as we both know, you are neither. Besides, having turned me hungry on to the streets, why should you care if a stranger offers me a meal?'

The words seemed to throb and echo in her head as she sat beside him in frozen silence for the remainder of the journey.

When they arrived back at the house, Sophie got out of the car before Angelo could come round to open the door for her, and ran inside to her room. She closed the door and leaned against it, shutting her eyes.

'*Why should you care? Why should you care?*' Over and over again, the question turned like a treadmill in her brain.

And she had no defences left, she thought bitterly. All her life, it seemed, she'd been trying to fight down this—agony which assailed her whenever Angelo became involved with a woman. Each time she deliberately referred to one of his loves, it had been like probing an open wound.

And, she knew, if Angelo responded to Nicole's invitation, or any other, then that wound would make her bleed to death.

Moving like an automaton, she undressed, showered, and put on one of the nightgowns Barbara had insisted she buy. It was sheer and sensuous, and for a moment, her courage almost failed her, and she hesitated, wondering if she should choose something less revealing.

Then castigated herself, because she knew that, whatever she was wearing, nothing could prevent the next few minutes from being the most difficult of her life, and she was simply delaying the inevitable.

She picked up the unicorn and held it in the palm of her hand. Her pledge, she thought. Her talisman.

And holding it tightly, she went out into the corridor and along the few yards which separated her room from his.

CHAPTER SEVEN

At his door, she hesitated again. Perhaps he was asleep. Or maybe he wasn't even there. She hadn't heard him pass her door. Instead of putting the car away, he could have driven back into Nassau—to Nicole. For a convulsive moment she pressed her clenched fist to her mouth, damning back the pain.

Then she opened the door and went in. The bedside lamp was on, and he was propped up on one elbow, reading a book. At the sound of the door, he lifted his head and looked at her, still keeping his place in the book, his brows raised in polite interrogation.

'What is it, Sophie? Can't you sleep?'

She shook her head. Her mouth was too dry to permit speech. She walked over to the bed and stood looking down at him for a long moment. Then, still in silence, she put the unicorn down on the pillow next to him.

His eyes examined the little figure, his face totally expressionless, then he picked it up, and put it, with his book, on the table beside the bed, before reaching out a hand and flipping back the sheet which was his only covering, indicating with a slight gesture that she should join him in bed.

She swallowed thickly and obeyed. Lying beside him, she wondered if she should have taken off her nightdress.

'At last,' he said quietly, 'Am I such a monster, Sophie?'

'No,' she said huskily.

'Then why are you trembling?'

She moistened her lips with the tip of her tongue. 'Because I'm nervous,' she said flatly. 'Because I've—never done this before, and I don't know what to expect—or what you'll expect of me . . .'

He said drily, 'I expect very little.' He paused. 'And not everything will be unfamiliar. This, for example . . .' He bent his head, and brushed her mouth softly with his. He gave her a faint, twisted smile. 'Was that so alarming?'

She shook her head. Her voice sounded piteous. 'I'm sorry. I'm such an idiot.'

'Perhaps,' he said. 'But not for the reasons you think.' He kissed her again, his lips lingering this time, coaxing hers to part a little, while his hand gently stroked her throat and shoulders. Whatever threat she had envisaged seemed to have withdrawn to a safe distance, and imperceptibly she began to relax, even to shyly return the warm, seeking pressure of his mouth.

His fingers caressed her softly, gliding down to where the tiny bodice of her nightdress skimmed her breasts, tracing their soft swell with a touch as light as a butterfly's wing. She felt him slide the straps of her nightdress off her shoulders, uncovering her, and knew a shock of swift, ungovernable pleasure as his hands touched her bare breasts, cupping, arousing with the gentle play of his fingers until the rosy nipples firmed into sweet, proud peaks.

He gave a murmur of satisfaction deep in this throat, then his head bent, and his mouth moved on her, engulfing her swollen flesh in liquid fire, his tongue teasing, tantalising, awakening her to a throbbing torment of the senses.

He kissed her mouth again, and this time she responded without reticence, welcoming the silken touch of his tongue against her own with breathless, innocent fervour. At the same time he lowered his body gently towards hers, creating a new, disturbing urgency as the hair-roughened muscular wall of his chest brushed her excited breasts. But so lightly, Sophie thought with a little inward moan, her body arching upwards, seeking him. Too lightly.

His hands closed on her again, with fierce purpose, the circular movements of his palms against the erect nipples sending swift tremors of something between pain and pleasure coursing through her being. She gasped, feverishly, restlessly, closing her eyes to escape the intensity of his dark gaze, the hooded eyes observing every slight fluctuation in the colour of her face, every convulsive movement of her throat muscles, every flutter of her eyelashes.

His hands left her breasts and began to stroke down her body, touching her without haste, exploring every curve and contour as if he was learning her through his fingertips. And where his fingers caressed, his mouth followed, turning her skin to flame, melting her bones, forcing little sounds from her throat.

And when the unhurried hand reached her thighs, gentling his way between them, she was already yielding, pliant and ready for this new and startling intimacy. As he caressed her, sensation rippled through her like a spring tide rising to the flood. There was a deep dark pleasure uncoiling inside her, slowly and inexorably as the long fingers stroked, coaxed and incited, taking her over and over again to some brink, then calling her back, controlling her reactions with total mastery.

He kissed her, his tongue stroking the sweet fullness of her lower lip, then lowered his mouth to her breasts once more, encircling each rosy tip in turn, tugging them gently with his lips, until Sophie cried out with a new abandonment.

Suddenly, the unknown was reaching out for her. The brink was there and this time there would be no recall, and she felt the last fragments of her self command slipping away as the pleasure inside her gathered to a pulsation which filled the world, splintering her in agony and delight.

And afterwards, she lay in silence on the shore where the tide had left her, and felt tears on her face.

She felt him move abruptly, then a click as the lamp was extinguished. For a bewildered moment she thought he was going to turn away from her and go to sleep, but in the darkness his arm went round her, drawing her against him, pillowing her head on his shoulder.

He said quietly, 'Sleep now, Sophie.'

Her bewilderment doubled. She lay staring into the darkness as questions tumbled round in her brain. She might be still comparatively innocent, but she wasn't dumb enough to think that was all there was to it. She was well aware that he'd made no attempt to satisfy his own needs, and yet he couldn't have been immune to what was taking place between them. She bit her lip. Perhaps she should make some move. Turn her head and kiss him perhaps. Or touch him—somewhere. Let him know that she was awake still, and—willing.

But she couldn't. In spite of what had just happened, or perhaps because of it, she was paralysed with shyness. He'd been her master every step of the way. She couldn't take the initiative now, especially as there wasn't the slightest hint that he wanted her to do so.

Lloyd Curzon's voice returned gratingly. *'Starting from square one must be a novelty for him.'* A novelty, she wondered with a kind of despair, or sheer excruciating boredom?

Perhaps he was so jaded that only experience could turn him on. She remembered that strange watchfulness, recalled how collected and in control he'd been all the time, and cringed inwardly. Maybe he'd found it amusing to observe her naïve responses, she thought desolately.

But somehow she had to know. She took her courage in both hands and said, 'Angelo?'

'Si.' His voice sounded cool, and not at all as if he had been summoned back from the borders of sleep.

She lay for a moment searching for the right words, some magic formula to convey what she wanted him to know. But there was nothing.

At last, she said feebly, 'I don't understand. Don't you—want to . . .? Because,' she hurried on wretchedly when he made no immediate reply. 'I—I don't mind. I mean—I'd like you to . . .' She stumbled to an appalled halt.

'*Grazie mille, mia cara.*' He sounded amused she realised with a pang. 'But—no. I think you have learned enough for this first time, don't you?'

Colour stormed into her face, and she wanted to burst into humiliated tears.

But instead she said, with an echo of his own coolness, 'Just as you wish. Shall I go back to my own room?'

'Would you find it easier to sleep?'

'I don't know.'

'Then stay here,' he said, and his arm tightened momentarily round her slender shoulders. 'Accustom yourself to one more new thing perhaps.'

But that, Sophie discovered, was easier said than done. She woke several times during the hours that followed, lying in the darkness, listening to his quiet even breathing, feeling the warmth of his naked body, close and relaxed next to her own, turning her face into his shoulder so that she could absorb the scent of his skin. All these things in turn sending their own potent signals to her brain, and curling along the nerve-endings of her newly awakened body.

He'd taught her to want him, she realised ruefully, and she'd learned that first, basic lesson only too well.

He was her husband, and only a few hours ago

he'd driven her almost insane in his arms, yet she still didn't have the confidence to obey her instincts, to kiss him to wakefulness, and let her mouth and hands tell him of her needs. Besides, she was terrified in case he laughed at her. She couldn't risk that drawling mockery in this situation. Or his forebearance either, she thought with sudden fierceness. And lay, aching to touch him, until weariness intervened once more, and she fell asleep.

The next time she awoke, it was daylight, and she was alone. She sat up slowly, looking round her, listening for some sound from the bathroom, but there was none. And it was late, she realised, catching sight of the small china clock, ticking gently away on the table beside the bed. Long past her usual time for getting up. Long past breakfast too.

And beside the clock was the unicorn. Sophie rolled across the bed and picked it up in her hand.

'This was not,' she told it softly, 'The bargain I expected.'

She bathed and dressed, and went rather hesitantly along to the living room where Nina was waiting to fuss round her with fruit juice, coffee and freshly baked rolls.

'Mist' Angelo said you were to have your sleep out,' she announced, beaming, obviously relieved that this eccentric honeymoon was following a more conventional pattern at last.

'Where is he?' Sophie tried to sound casual.

'Oh, he took the car and went into Nassau,'

Nina said cheerfully 'He'll be back any time now.'

'I see.' Sophie pushed aside the remains of her roll, and got up, smiling stiffly. 'I'm not 'really very hungry. I think I'll—go for a swim.'

She walked through the gardens and down to the beach, her hands clenched into fists in the pockets of her tunic, her mind working overtime. She rejected instantly the idea that Angelo's trip to Nassau could possibly be connected with the sultry Nicole, but it kept coming back to torment her just the same.

And she hadn't expected to wake up alone, and be told that he'd gone off in the car, just the same as if this was any other morning. Yet that was probably exactly what it was to him, she thought, her teeth sinking into the soft flesh inside her lower lip. Just another day, after just another night . . .

She peeled off the tunic and ran into the sea, welcoming its cool silkiness against her skin. She submerged quickly and began to swim, exercising strongly, not floating and playing as she usually did. Her arms and legs felt heavy with weariness as she eventually turned back towards the shore.

Angelo was waiting for her as she walked slowly through the shallows.

'*Buon giorno, carissima.*' His voice was teasing. 'Are you in training for the next Olympics, perhaps.'

'No,' Sophie said shortly, not looking at him. She picked up her towel, and began to blot the excess moisture from her arms and shoulders. 'I just felt like swimming. Heaven knows there's little else to do around here.'

There was a silence, then Angelo said coolly, 'Then perhaps you would not object too strongly if our stay here was curtailed. There are matters in London which require my attention, and then I should go to New York.'

Sophie shrugged. 'That suits me perfectly well,' she said. 'Do—do you want me to pack for you.'

His brows lifted. 'How very domesticated of you, *mia bella*. But I think Nina can be safely trusted to perform that service for us both. Now, if you will excuse me, I have some paperwork to attend to.'

Sophie nodded, and stood her ground drying herself until his tall figure had disappeared. Then she sank down on the rug spread in the shade of the sun umbrella, and covered her face with her hands.

So—the honeymoon was over, she thought desolately. And it demonstrated quite forcibly that she had no power to hold his interest sexually. Young and healthy, she thought. A suitable wife to sit at his dinner table. A suitable mother for his children. Well brought up, malleable, and dull.

Well, he'd never pretended there was anything more to it than that, and his indifference to her initial refusal to be a wife to him should have warned her, she thought wretchedly. Besides, what more could she realistically expect when she'd married him on the rebound anyway, and he knew it . . .

She stopped with a little gasp, as she realised how long it was since she'd even given Mark and his betrayal a second thought. Since that awful day on Avirenze, it had been Angelo, taking over her life, filling her thoughts to the exclusion of everyone else, making her too angry, too alive to mourn for her lost love. Making her wonder just how much that love had really meant to her . . .

But that was ridiculous, she told herself fiercely. Because anything else made no sense, no sense at all.

The day passed slowly. Nina and Simeon were clearly disappointed that they were leaving, and Nina elected to cook a special farewell dinner, in spite of Sophie's protests.

'I'd like to do it,' she said firmly. 'And you and Mist' Angelo have got to come back, you hear? And bring the babies,' she added with a broad grin.

The meal was wonderful. Angelo ate well, and congratulated Nina warmly, but he had seemed preoccupied, Sophie thought, toying with her dessert. Some banking problem, no doubt, and something she would have to get used to. That, among other things . . .

Back in the living room, she poured Angelo's coffee as she'd done each evening, but refused any herself.

'We have a long flight tomorrow,' she made herself say casually. 'I think I'll go to my room.'

'As you wish.' As she passed him, he caught her hand, detaining her. He said softly, 'May I come to you tonight?'

Startled colour rose in her face. She said, half-stammering, 'Actually, I have a slight headache. The sun, I think . . .'

'I see,' he said. He lifted the hand he held to his lips, bestowing a swift formal kiss. 'Then good night, *mia cara*, and sleep well.'

She would be lucky if she closed her eyes, she thought. Her room was a depressing sight, with the luggage packed and ready, and one case waiting for her night things and the few final items. She undressed slowly, and took a leisurely bath before getting into bed. She switched off the lamp, and stretched out, thinking idly how quiet the house seemed. Perhaps everyone was creeping about out of consideration for her non-existent headache.

She turned restlessly, and as she did so, she heard it—the unmistakable sound of the car starting up and driving away. She sank back against the pillows, pressing a hand to her mouth. This time there could be no doubt about where he was going, or to whom, and pain slashed at her.

She buried her face in the pillow, choking back the sobs which rose in her throat. Perhaps there would come a time when she could ignore or accept this kind of casual infidelity from him, but if so, that time was not yet. Sophie had never taken a sleeping pill in her life, but she longed for one now—something to bring oblivion until morning at least.

She didn't hear the sound of the door opening. The first realisation that she was no longer alone came when the bedside light snapped on. She sat up, clutching the sheet to her breasts, and pushing the tumbled hair out of her eyes.

Angelo was standing by the bed. He was

wearing the red silk dressing gown she remembered from that night at Bishops Wharton, and was carrying a glass containing some cloudy liquid.

She said incredulously. 'You? But I heard the car . . .'

He smiled at her. 'I gave it to Nina and Simeon for the rest of the night, and some money too to enjoy as they wish in Nassau. A small thanks for the way they have looked after us.'

Sophie fiddled with the edge of the sheet. 'That was—kind.'

'I can be kinder still.' He offered her the glass. 'Some soluble aspirin, *mia cara*, for your headache.'

'Thank you.' Sophie moistened her lips with the tip of her tongue. 'But it's better.'

'I am delighted to hear it,' he said silkily. 'So—there is nothing to prevent my joining you to—er consummate our marriage?'

As Sophie gaped at him, he went on, 'It is a formality I think we should observe before we leave here, and I had the impression last night that you agreed. Was I wrong?'

'No,' she managed somehow.

'Good.' He put the glass down beside the bed, then leaned calmly across and twitched the sheet from Sophie's nerveless fingers, tossing it down to the foot of the bed.

She gave a little outraged cry and dived to retrieve it, but Angelo forestalled her, half-kneeling on the bed, his hand clasping her wrists to restrain her.

'*Per Dio*, Sophie, what now?' He sounded

exasperated. 'Surely you cannot be embarrassed to have me look at you?'

'Yes, I can,' she said fiercely. 'I'm just not used to . . .'

'Sophie,' he said gently, releasing her wrists. 'Last night in my arms, there was not an inch of you I did not touch or kiss. The room was not dark, nor were my eyes closed. So—what is the difference?'

'I don't know.' She didn't look at him. 'But there is one.'

There was a silence, then he sighed. 'I shall have to take your word for that, *mia bella*.' He reached down and drew the sheet back over her body. 'So—modesty is restored. I will not look at you, since that is your wish, and nor will I require you to look at me.' He switched off the lamp. She heard the rustle of his robe as he removed it. Then the movement of the bed as he came to lie beside her.

His hands began to touch her lightly, triggering with almost shocking immediacy all those newly-learned responses. She recognised tremblingly the change in her own breathing, the unerring clamour of blood and senses. Irresistible, she thought with a kind of despair. As if, God help her, she'd been programmed . . .

Angelo kissed her then, not persuasively as he had the previous night, but with a frank sensual hunger which she realised dimly she could share, or not, as she chose. Only, the choice was no longer hers to make.

His cool hands stroked and moulded their way down her body, enticing her beyond mere surrender to new dimensions of need, creating possibilities of pleasure she could hardly comprehend. She bit back the little moan of wanting, rising in her throat. Snatched at the remnants of self-control, forcing herself to lie passive in his arms.

His hand found the moist warmth of her, paused, goading, tantalising.

He said, 'Tell me what you want, Sophie. This?' His fingers moved, silkily, rhythmically, shattering that fragile control. 'And—this?'

Her body arched in demand, and in welcome. 'Yes, damn you—oh, yes.'

She hardly recognised her own voice. She was involved in a sharp, sweet intensity, feeling it gather her inexorably into a spiral of almost painful delight. And in the midst of it, from some recess of consciousness, she felt him move, felt a burning pressure, a swift momentary spasm of pain, then a heated increase in sensation within her, and all around her. With a sob, she reached for it, strained after it, and fell, shuddering into some deep and ageless void.

She came back slowly to full awareness of the room, the darkness, the man beside her, no longer part of her, or even touching. She moved slightly, languidly, recognising an unfamiliar but not unpleasant ache.

He said with cool politeness, 'I hope I did not hurt you too badly.'

'No,' Sophie said, stammering a little. 'Oh, no.' There were other things she knew she should say—wanted to say. Things which would express her gratitude, and more than that.

She wanted to tell him that she loved him.

The realisation jolted her back instantly to horrified reality. Her body was clammy with perspiration, her heart thudding so violently she was almost amazed he couldn't hear it.

It isn't true, she thought desperately, clawing at some kind of sanity. It couldn't be true.

It was a delusion—some lingering aftermath from the world of sensual pleasure he had unlocked for her. Some flare-up from that old, childhood crush when she'd transformed him from human being into fantasy hero.

But no more. He'd demonstrated unequivocally that he was flesh and blood, turning those adolescent dreams into devastating fact. Imagination had never taken her so far, or so fast, she thought dazedly.

But none of it added up to love, she thought fiercely, dragging herself back from the edge of the abyss.

And there had not been word from him, she reminded herself. Not one caress, or endearment, just that courteous enquiry after her well-being.

But, of course, that had not been in the terms of their marriage she thought. And she could imagine his reaction, if she was to stammer out some naïve confession of devotion. He would certainly be amused. He might even be embarrassed—and kind.

And she could not bear it if he was kind.

His hand stroked her arm, and in spite of her morass of emotional confusion, she felt every nerve-ending warm and tingle at the soft brush of his hand over her skin.

She tensed in rigidity and rejection.

Her voice sounded slightly choked. 'Please—not again.'

The questing hand stilled, and was withdrawn.

'As you wish.' Polite, again, and totally unperturbed. He might even have been smiling. 'Sleep well, *carissima*.'

She felt him move, thought he was turning away from her to sleep, then realised he was out of bed, and heard the brief sounds in the darkness that told her he was putting on his robe. Heard, too, his tread going away from her across the room, and the slight creak of the door as he left.

She wanted to call after him, but she did not dare. The fear of what words she might find on her lips, what she might betray, kept her silent.

She lay, staring into the darkness, trying to come to terms with all kinds of things, of which loneliness was only the first. Loneliness was inevitable, she thought wretchedly, born out of the necessity for reticence about her deepest feelings. And the old hostility and wariness had been easier barriers to erect in her mind against him.

It had been that sudden passion of jealousy she'd experienced when she'd accused him of having an *affaire* with Vanessa Carter which had first alerted her to what the truth of her feelings might be, although she'd fought to dismiss it as an absurdity.

And it was still absurd, she told herself wearily. There was no mileage in loving Angelo. He wanted the convenience of a wife at his side, to act as his hostess, and ultimately to mother his children. A suitable, practical arrangement from all points of view, with no emotional ties or obligations to cloud it. And making love to his wife, turning her into a willing bed-partner was yet another convenience. And when, in time, he wanted more than duty sex, he would look for passion and excitement elsewhere.

The thought wrenched at her like an iron claw, and she turned her face into her pillow, stifling a whimper.

The honeymoon, such as it had been, was over.

CHAPTER EIGHT

SOPHIE leaned forward and tapped on the glass which divided the rear of the car from the driver.

She said, as the chauffeur inclined his head, 'Will you stop please. I'd like to walk for a while. Do some window shopping.'

He pulled over to the kerb, and Fabrizio, who was sitting beside him, came round to open the door for her. She thanked him with a slight smile as she stepped out on to the pavement.

She was accustomed to having him there, a few steps in the rear, now, although at first she'd been inclined to rebel against the necessity. She'd accepted too that although on Avirenze, Fabrizio might act as a secretary, here in New York and the other cities where Angelo had a *pied à terre*, he was a bodyguard. She didn't ask if he might be armed, because she didn't want to know. If he had to be there, she was glad it was someone she liked, and was used to.

The wind was cold, and she huddled into the warmth of her sable coat, with a faint shiver. Thanksgiving was behind them, and Christmas on its way, and although there hadn't been snow as yet, it was on its way too.

Angelo had not told her whether they would be spending Christmas in New York, but she thought it was unlikely. It was probable that they would take up her parents' invitation to join them at Bishops Wharton for the festivities.

Angelo, at least, would assume that was what she wanted. But Sophie wasn't so sure. Barbara was eagle-eyed and shrewd, and Sophie wasn't convinced she could keep up the pretence of newly-wedded bliss for any length of time.

It had been difficult enough on their previous, brief visit to behave like a normal, happily besotted bride, and anyway, they'd stayed in London, and not at the house. At Christmas, they would be expected to share a room, which would cause problems.

She stopped, staring unseeingly at a lavish window display of glossily expensive luggage.

For the fact was that apart from that one occasion on their honeymoon, Angelo had never spent an entire night with her, and that the pattern of them having separate rooms had been continued, first in London, and now at their New York apartment.

And what Lucia, who, with her husband Guiseppe, looked after them there, thought about it, Sophie hadn't the slightest idea.

Angelo had told her casually that he had permanent staff at the apartment, but had said nothing more. He'd left her to discover Lucia for herself.

Sophie, who'd been expecting the usual formality of the correctly trained servant, had been frankly stunned when this overweight whirlwind with grizzled hair, and a smile as wide as the world had burst upon her, and gathered her to her bosom in a flood of excited Italian.

And she'd been frankly amazed when Lucia
had rounded on him, ordering him not to look so
pleased with himself.

'All these years I have been telling you it is
time you got married, and at last you take my
advice, but not before time,' she told him loudly,
and Angelo grinned back at her with more
affection, Sophie thought with a pang, than she'
had ever seen him show anyone.

'Better late than never, you shrew,' he retorted.
'Where is Guiseppe, or have you nagged him into
his grave?'

'He is—somewhere.' Lucia shrugged her dis-
regard for the entire male sex, her dark eyes fixed
on Sophie's jet-lagged pallor. 'It is time you
rested, *Signora*, and I will bring you a cup of my
good soup,' she ordained briskly.

With a sense of wonderment, Sophie found
herself being helped out of her dress and shoes,
and under the covers of the huge bed in the
master bedroom. With less wonderment, she
learned that Lucia had been Angelo's nurse.

'It is difficult to exact the proper respect from
her, when you know she pinned on your first
napkins,' Angelo told her ruefully later. 'But she
loves my family with a devotion no money can ever
buy. She will love you too, *mia cara*,' he added,
half-laughing. 'I hope you can stand up to it.'

As Lucia was prone to express forthright
opinions on all subjects, Sophie was surprised
and relieved when she made no comment on the
separate rooms issue. Perhaps she realised it was
dangerous ground, even for someone with her
privileged status.

Guiseppe turned out to be a small twinkling man, completely under his wife's thumb, and apparently more than content for it to be so.

Lucia had commented only once on Sophie's relationship with her husband, and that was during their first days in New York.

'It is good the *Signor* has taken a wife,' she had told Sophie almost abruptly. 'He works so hard—too hard often, and does not relax, so he gets thin.' Her eyes twinkled suddenly. 'So—I feed him good, and you love him good, and between us we fix that. And when the *bambinos* come, I look after them too,' she added, giving Sophie a slight dig in the ribs.

Sophie had flushed and muttered something in reply. But the fact was after six months of marriage, there was still no sign of a child—a fact that like so much else was never mentioned between them.

Sophie sighed, and aware that Fabrizio was becoming slightly restive, moved on to the jewellery store next door. It was interesting she thought to reflect that she could have gone into the store and ordered any of the fabulous settings of gold and precious stones on show in the window without turning a hair. The allowance which Angelo made her each quarter was more than lavish, and she never spent a third of it. And even if she'd been tempted, she would probably have resisted, recognising how little he asked in return.

She sighed again, and walked on.

She looked at herself in the next shop window. Attractive, she thought judiciously, blonde hair piled on top of her head, wrapped in expensive furs. No longer a child, with a woman's knowledge in her eyes, a woman's fulfilment adding mystery to her expression. For which she had Angelo to thank.

When he came to her room—which was by no means every night, she had to acknowledge—he was endlessly generous, erotically inventive about the ways in which he gave her pleasure.

But, and the admission gave her no pleasure at all, it was all totally one-sided. His own satisfaction was brief, almost perfunctory, achieved, she sometimes believed, as an after-thought.

For while she had fallen in love with her husband physically as well as emotionally, there was nothing to suggest that he was in any way involved with her to the same extent.

She had little to go on, of course. But she'd seen Mark with Vanessa Carter, seen him oblivious, blinded by passion to everything else in the world while he was possessing her.

But Angelo . . . Sophie bit her lip. When he took her, it was swift, almost clinical, the situation, she thought bitterly, never for one moment out of that superhuman control. And he never, ever spent the night with her.

They shared a bathroom, but none of the usual intimacies. She had never seen him shave. He had never washed her back when she bathed. In fact, he was almost studious in the way he kept from intruding on her privacy.

And any shy overtures she was prompted to make, he appeared not to notice.

Last night had been a case in point. They'd been at the theatre together—a Broadway first night, and a certain hit judging by the reaction of the audience. But it could have been a touring rep's revival of some third rate farce for all Sophie knew. All she'd been conscious of was Angelo sitting next to her, his thigh inches from her own. She'd wanted so badly for him to turn his head, meet her eyes, smile at her in anticipation and promise. But his entire attention was fixed on the stage.

Later, as they drove back to the apartment in the limousine, she wondered to herself what he would do if she made a direct advance to him. Tempted him with some of the things he'd taught her in the darkness of her room. Would he order the chauffeur to drive round the Park, or, as was far more likely, would he remind her politely that they were not alone.

Lucia and Guiseppe had been told not to wait up, so they had the apartment to themselves. There was the usual pot of coffee waiting for them on a small electric hob, and a covered dish of sandwiches.

She said lightly, 'Lucia seems to think we're always in imminent danger of starvation.'

He was pouring himself some coffee. 'Would you like some perhaps?'

She shook her head. 'I'd never sleep,' she excused herself not altogether truthfully. She dropped her wrap on to the chesterfield and walked towards him. 'Could you help.' She kept her voice level. 'This stupid zip always sticks.'

'Of course.' She felt his hands at the back of

her dress, the downward glide of the fastener from the neck to its ultimate limit. He said drily, 'Not such a problem, after all. Good night, Sophie, and sleep well.'

She was thankful her back was turned to him, and that he could not read the disappointment, the chagrin in her face.

She said quietly, 'Good night. It's been a wonderful evening,' and went to her room, to lie for hours tossing and turning alone.

Well, she'd made the rules, she told herself in bitter self-derision, and she had only herself to blame if now he insisted on keeping them, and if, as a consequence, she spent so many nights alone, aching for him.

Of course, there was nothing to prevent her going to him, except cowardice. She no longer had the little unicorn as an excuse. It had vanished completely, and she was shy about enquiring over its whereabouts. It was altogether too fraught a symbol for casual questioning. But she wished endlessly it was back in her possession.

It seemed there was no other way she could approach him. Because except for the hours when he held her in his arms, they could have been two strangers sharing the same roof. Angelo was invariably polite, but always remote, that air of aloof arrogance which Sophie remembered from her earliest acquaintance with him effectively keeping her at a distance.

And she wouldn't even let herself consider where he might spend the nights he was apart from her.

She shivered. She was tired of looking in store windows at items she had not the least intention of buying. She might as well go back to the apartment, she thought restlessly. There was a selection of the latest novels awaiting her there, as well as the embroidery she was now beginning to enjoy—and, of course, the ceaseless anodyne of television.

She turned away abruptly, nearly cannoning into someone standing just behind her as she did so. She recoiled with a little gasp, and a murmur of apology, and was about to move on when a hand grasped her arm, and a voice she had never expected to hear again said urgently, 'Sophie? My God, it is you.'

She said on a note of disbelief. 'Mark? But it can't be . . .'

Over his shoulder, she saw Fabrizio moving towards them, an ugly expression on his face, and she lifted a hand. 'It's all right, Fabrizio.' She was amazed to hear how steady her voice sounded. She gave Mark a cool smile. 'What a surprise. I had no idea you were in New York.'

He looked affluent, she couldn't help noticing, with an elegant top coat covering his conventional grey suit.

He said almost dismissively, 'I came for a conference—to represent Jeffersons.'

She frowned in sudden bewilderment. 'Then Craig took you on after all?'

'Of course,' Mark said. 'He had no reason not to.'

'But the money,' she began.

His smile sneered. 'You mean he never told

you? Well, I suppose I can understand that. It can't be very nice for a new bride to be told she's just been sold to you like any other commodity.'

He looked down at her, and his expression changed. 'God, you look beautiful,' he said huskily. 'No wonder he wanted you.' He shuddered. 'I told myself that it would all be for nothing. That you hated him. That you'd never go through with it. I thought I'd die when I read the papers and saw you'd actually married him.' His eyes were tormented as they looked into hers. 'I've had nightmares—do you know that? Over and over again I've imagined that bastard—with you—having you.'

Colour stormed into Sophie's pale cheeks, She said tautly, 'Please don't speak of my husband in those terms. And be thankful you've only had your imagination to contend with. You've never actually stood and watched as I did . . .'

Mark's face was remorseful. 'I'm sorry,' he muttered unevenly. 'I know I shouldn't say these things, but seeing you like this has brought it all back to me. How could I have been such a fool as to let you go?'

Sophie bit her lip. 'I really don't think I want to pursue this discussion. We can't recall the past.'

But Mark stood his ground. 'Oh, you really belong to him, don't you,' he said softly. 'You warned me what a ruthless swine he could be, and I took no notice. I let him sucker me into going to Avirenze, and when I got there, he delivered the ultimatum.'

Sophie shook her head. 'I don't know what

you're talking about, and I really ought to be going . . .'

'You have to listen to me,' he insisted almost hoarsely. 'Walk with me a little way.'

'There's no point,' Sophie protested, feeling intensely uncomfortable. 'I don't need any explanations, Mark. Besides, it's far too late.'

'Too late,' Mark said quietly. 'Because you're now Mrs Angelo Marchese with all that means. And you could have been mine.'

Sophie gave him a look compounded of amazement and resentment. 'I was yours,' she said angrily. 'If you recall, it was you who had other ideas.'

'You mean my wild *affaire* with Vanessa?' he asked almost contemptuously. 'The big set-up of the century, orchestrated and stage managed by Angelo Marchese himself?'

'Hardly a set-up.' Sophie faced him with it. 'After all I did catch you together.'

'You were meant to,' he said. 'If not then, at some other time. You see, you had to be so disgusted with me that you'd send me away of your own free will. That you'd never want to see me again. I thought the gossip about Vanessa and me would get back to you, and the bust-up would come that way. But no-one told you anything. They were all trying to protect you.'

She said, 'You're still not making any sense.'

'That first night on Avirenze,' Mark's voice was low and intense. 'Your cousin came to me. He was furious about your announcement that we were engaged. He told me that I would never be allowed to marry you, but that I could have the money I wanted for the Jefferson partnership, and more besides if I'd behave in such a way that you'd throw me over for good.' He paused. 'He said he didn't give a damn how I did it, but I had to make you fall out of love with me.' He swallowed. 'Then he told me—that he was going to marry you himself. He said he'd chosen you years before, but nothing has ever been said to you because he wasn't ready to settle down. And he wanted you delivered to him wrapped up, and brand new.' He paused again, letting everything he'd said sink into her startled consciousness. 'God forgive me, Sophie, I—hated him for that. The thought of letting you go—to him—made me sick to my stomach. I wanted you so damned badly myself. That's why I lost my head that time I actually managed to be alone with you.' He sighed. 'But even then he won.'

She said slowly, 'If all this is true, why didn't you tell me? Why did you just give in?'

'He said if I even thought of it, then he'd make sure I never worked again for the rest of my life. I could choose, Sophie. The career I wanted, or a lifetime spent hanging round the Job Centre. Well, I'd had some of that. I couldn't face it again. And I couldn't ask you to face it with me either. He knew that,' he added bitterly.

She was shaking like a leaf. 'You didn't have a great deal faith in me.'

'What good is faith when you have nothing else to offer,' he said in a low voice. 'I had nothing, Sophie, and he knew it, and he was going to make sure it stayed that way unless I did what he wanted.' He groaned. 'And even faith took a beating when I read about your wedding in the newspapers. I couldn't believe it. You always claimed you hated the guy, yet you dropped into his hand like a ripe plum. How could you do that?'

'Because I was unhappy,' she said huskily. 'Because at the time, it seemed the only thing left to me. I didn't realise . . .' She paused, colour swamping her face again.

'How could you?' Mark said, totally mis-interpreting her halting words. 'You understand, Sophie, why I had to tell you all this. I could hardly believe my luck when I saw you standing there. I just couldn't go on knowing that you hated me for what I'd done.'

He tried to take her hand, but she stepped back instinctively, putting herself out of range. She said quietly, 'No, I don't hate you, Mark. You did what you felt you had to do. So did I. Perhaps it hasn't turned out quite how we thought for either of us. Now, my car's waiting. Goodbye.'

She left him and walked rapidly to the kerb. Fabrizio was there ahead of her to open the door and assist her into the rear seat, his face unusually grim and stony as he did so.

But Sophie hardly noticed. She was feeling too grim and stony herself, a flame of rage burning up inside her and threatening to break into a conflagration.

She sat in silence all the way back to the apartment, her mind turning over and over everything Mark had said with a kind of stupefied horror. He'd treated her despicably—

but the fact that he'd apparently done it to order made it all a hundred times worse.

John, her stepfather whom she loved, and Angelo, working hand in glove to cold-bloodedly rid themselves of the young man who was proving an obstacle to their plans. All the time she'd been growing up, she'd been groomed for her future marriage to Angelo only she hadn't realised it. School, Switzerland, everything training her for her role as Angelo's wife.

Her nails bit into the palms of her hands. 'And I didn't even know I was in the audition,' she thought bitterly.

She walked past the commissionaire without returning his friendly greeting, and went straight up to the apartment in the elevator. Once in the living room, she took off her sable coat and threw it on the floor in a way which would have shocked Lucia, if she'd been there to see it, but she was out shopping.

'Part of my bride price,' Sophie thought, shame scorching along her veins. 'Oh God, how could he? How *dared* he?'

She walked restlessly up and down, remembering everything that had happened between them in minute detail, feeding her inward rage as she did so. God, how easily she'd been duped. And the callous way it had been done. She shuddered violently, then picked up a small china ornament from the table beside the chesterfield and hurled it into the fireplace, smashing it to bits.

She heard footsteps approaching down the passage and tensed. Lucia must have returned, and was coming to investigate the noise. She could hardly say it was an accident, so she would have to brazen it out, she thought, swinging round towards the opening door, her chin already lifting defiantly.

But it was Angelo who stood in the doorway. For a moment, she was too surprised to speak or move. He was home hours before he should have been.

His dark eyes flicked over her, taking in everything—her rigidity, the tumbled coat on the floor, the damage in the fireplace.

He said coolly, 'If you intend to continue with this destructive phase, Sophie, may I suggest the blue vase. I have never cared for it.'

She said in a small high voice, 'What are you doing here? Oh, I suppose Fabrizio told you . . .'

'About your—unexpected encounter in the avenue? Yes, of course he did.'

Her voice shook. 'I suppose you thought I'd never see him again. That I'd never find out what you did—that disgusting, *loathsome* bargain you made with him.'

His brows lifted. 'Hard words, Sophie, to describe just another business transaction.'

She gasped. 'Is that how you describe— breaking my heart?'

His mouth twisted sardonically. 'I don't think I did that, *mia cara*,' he said unpardonably. 'Although I may have dented your pride a little.'

She grabbed for another ornament, realised with chagrin that it was in fact the blue vase, but threw it anyway, straight at his head. But she was well wide of the mark, and the vase crashed in fragments against the door behind him.

'If you wish to conduct a quarrel on these terms, *bella mia*, you will have to improve your aim.' He sounded almost bored. He walked forward. 'On the other hand, you could sit down with me and listen to what I have to say.'

'You can go to hell.' Her breasts were rising and falling stormily. 'Do you think I'd ever believe another word you said. Mark told me everything—how you bribed him—threatened him with ruin—forced him into an *affaire* with that Carter bitch so that I'd be compelled to break off our engagement.'

Angelo actually laughed. 'Is that what he told you? That Carter bitch as you so aptly describe her, *carissima*, can make all her own running. She needs no assistance from me, believe me. And Mark, I am informed, was only too willing to co-operate. If he finds computers are not his vocation after all, he could probably make a good living as a rich women's stud.' He shrugged. 'Don't tear yourself in pieces, Sophie. Mark had his price, and I paid it. There was no more to it than that.'

'No more?' Sophie repeated. 'No more?' Her voice rose to a shout. 'You can stand there and say that. You didn't just pay off Mark, you bastard. You bought me. Oh God, *you bought me*.'

She saw his face change. No trace of amusement, if there ever had been. No patience either. Suddenly—an anger as deep as her own, mingled with another element which sent her, dry-mouthed, backwards away from him, frightened that the situation was out of her control.

He walked towards her slowly, the dark eyes glittering brilliantly, dangerously into hers as he moved. There was nowhere for her to retreat any more. No way to escape the terrifying purpose in his face.

He said almost silkily. 'So I bought you. If I did, then so far, God knows, I have seen little enough return for my money.'

He reached for her, picking her up in his arms, and carrying her across the room to the door. Sophie almost crying with rage and swift fear pummelled his chest with clenched fists.

'Put me down, damn you. Oh God, I hate you . . .'

'Hate me all you want,' he said, and there was a note in his voice which choked all further words in her throat. 'It can only be an advance on the passive submission I usually endure from you.'

He carried her into her bedroom, kicking the door shut behind him before walking over and dropping her in the centre of the massive bed.

He knelt over her, pinioning her writhing body ruthlessly between his thighs, ignoring the futile blows she aimed at him. He took the neckline of her dress in his hands and tore it slowly and deliberately from throat to hem.

She was very still suddenly, her eyes widening endlessly as she looked up into his face. She said, 'No—you can't . . .'

'Why not? I paid for the dress too. And for these charming trifles you wear under it.' With a quick movement, he wrenched the fragile lace cups of her bra apart. His hands moved down, ripping her lacy briefs as if they were paper.

Sophie said hoarsely. 'Angelo—please. Not like this . . .'

He shrugged, unfastening his belt. 'Unfortunately, my unwilling bride, you no longer have a choice. You've kept me at a distance long enough.' He gave a soft, cynical laugh. 'My beautiful wife—the one woman I could never reach. It is almost comic, don't you think?'

He entered her without preliminaries, without one kiss, one caress, any of the lingering, erotic arousal to which he had so sweetly attuned her body.

She lay, dazed and mute, knowing for the first time the full bitterness of being used without tenderness or consideration. No worse, she tried to tell herself over and over again, than many women had to suffer most of their lives. And yet, from Angelo, it seemed a violation not merely of her body but of her soul too.

The skilful lover to whom her pleasure had been the prime concern had vanished. In his place was an angry, bitter stranger caring only for his own satisfaction as he drove harshly into her body, as if he was exorcising some private demon of frustration and despair.

And this, Sophie recognised, was no time to protest, to tell him that he was wrong. There was an abyss of misunderstanding yawning between them, but somehow, when this nightmare of bitterness was over, she would find some way to traverse it. To tell him, at last, that she loved him and needed him, and that there was nothing to keep them apart any longer.

At last—at long last, her ordeal was over. She

felt his body shudder violently, heard his harsh cry, then he collapsed pulling himself away from her, his breathing fast and ragged. She turned her head and looked at him, lying with his face buried in his folded arms, then put out a hand and touched his cheek very gently.

He moved then, but not turning to her as she had hoped. Instead he brushed her hand away almost impatiently, then pulled himself into a sitting position, raking back his dishevelled hair.

He looked at Sophie, the dark eyes steely and inflexible as they surveyed her trembling body, the wide tearless eyes in her pale face.

He said softly, 'Don't move, my beautiful one. I have not finished with you yet.'

She watched him walk to the door, and lock it, then come back towards the bed, almost casually shedding his clothes as he did so.

He lifted Sophie slightly, setting her down among the pillows, sweeping away her ruined clothes to the floor with a careless gesture before joining her. She searched his face, looking for some trace of warmth, some semblance of his usual gentleness towards her, but there was nothing for her comfort at all.

He lifted her hand and brushed it with his lips in a cruel parody of his normal courtesy. He said, 'Well, *carissima*? Is everything now clear to you? You appreciate that from now I shall take you whenever and however I wish, and you may co-operate or not—as you wish,' he added bitingly.

There was an agony of weeping twisting inside her, but she did not let it show. She said steadily enough. 'You don't mean that. You can't mean it.'

'You think not?' He touched her crudely, insolently. 'Well, I have the whole evening and the whole night ahead of us to prove you wrong, *mia cara*.' He smiled slowly and humourlessly. 'But don't look so stricken, my sweet one. Who knows? By morning, I may be tired of you anyway.' He watched her flinch and laughed. 'Just think, Sophie, a few hours endurance and you could be spared my filthy lusts forever. You can revert to being the well-dressed presence at my side on social occasions, and I can find a woman who actually wants me in her bed.' He laughed again, pulling her towards him. 'But until then, *carissima*,' he made the endearment sound like an insult. 'I'll get my money's worth from you.'

CHAPTER NINE

THE room was still dark when she crawled back to consciousness, but something told her that it was broad daylight beyond the drapes, and probably closer to noon than breakfast time.

She was alone, and had probably been so for some time, she thought, propping herself up on one elbow, although she hadn't been aware of him leaving her.

She moved warily, flexing aching muscles, some of which she was sure she'd never used before. Some of which, she thought wrily, she'd not even been aware she possessed.

She sighed, feeling a sudden warmth steal into her face at the thought, and lay back against the pillows. Certainly, she could never accuse Angelo of making idle threats, she decided ruefully. He had—entertained himself with her most of the night, hardly allowing her any sleep, or even a breathing space. In a few incredible hours she had been taught swiftly and unequivocally more about pleasing a man than she could have expected to learn in a lifetime.

Her colour deepened helplessly as some memories began to filter back to her. A small wry smile curved her mouth. Well—she'd wondered many times during the past six months just what it would take to blow his cool, shatter that immaculate reserve forever, and now she knew.

He could never be aloof with her again, she told herself with satisfaction, not now that she was as intimately acquainted with every inch of his magnificent body as she'd ever been with her own. Not now that one stringent, breathless lesson had shown her exactly how and where he liked to be kissed—caressed.

Her smile widened into a grin. 'From now on—putty in my hands,' she airily told the room at large. Nor was he tired of her. Her final memory before she'd fallen asleep from sheer exhaustion had been his voice saying her name like a prayer.

Sophie stretched luxuriously. She would find ways of keeping his interest in her alive and well, she promised herself. Perhaps she'd begin by giving Lucia and Guiseppe the night off, and welcoming him home wearing nothing but the sable coat.

Perhaps he hadn't even gone to the bank's offices today. Maybe he'd gone off to his own room to recover too.

She pushed back the covers, and slid out of bed, looking critically down at herself. She wasn't bruised. His treatment of her had stopped a long way short of brutality, but there were faint marks on her skin.

Honourable scars she told herself as she put on her robe.

She could hear the faint whine of the vacuum cleaner as she made her way to his room. Lucia was cleaning the living room, she guessed, as she tried Angelo's door.

But the drapes were back, filling it with wintry

sunlight, and showing her quite clearly that it was unoccupied, the bed smooth in pristine order. In fact the whole place had a bare, almost spartan look, Sophie thought with sudden puzzlement. She saw something glinting on the floor where the sun's rays were catching it, and bent down to see what it was, straightening with a cry of distress.

In her hand she held the little glass unicorn, snapped in two.

'Oh, no,' she mourned cradling it pitifully in her palm, trying to fight off the feeling of unease which was beginning to assail her. Today of all days, he might have stayed with her, letting her wake up in his arms. Letting her put her lips on his as she told him she loved him. Last night there'd been no opportunity to tell him what was in her heart. He'd been in no mood to listen she recalled, silencing her peremptorily with his mouth every time she attempted even a few halting words.

But this was to be a new day, the beginning of their real marriage, with all bitterness, all misunderstanding cleared out of their lives.

Finding her beloved unicorn broken on the floor seemed like the worst of all omens.

She put the fragments down sorrowfully upon the polished surface of a tallboy, and left the room.

Lucia who was putting her cleaning things away hailed her. 'I didn't wake you, I hope. The *Signor* said you should sleep on as long as possible. He would not even disturb you to say goodbye, but left you a letter instead.'

Sophie stared at her. 'That's rather extreme, isn't it?' she asked. 'After all, he'll be home this evening.'

It was Lucia's turn to stare. 'Ah, no, *Signora*. Did you not know. The *Signor* has to make a trip to the Middle East. I had to pack for him—oh, very early this morning. His plane will have left by now.'

Sophie felt stunned. 'No, I had no idea,' she managed, quite creditably. 'I suppose that's why he came home so early yesterday afternoon, to tell me about it.'

Luica shrugged. 'And he forgot? *Non importa*. He will be back very soon, I think.' She gave Sophie one of her beaming smiles. 'And now I make you some breakfast?'

'Just coffee, please.' She was beginning to feel badly frightened now. 'And—where is my letter, Lucia?'

'I left it on the mantel above the fireplace,' Luica called back as she went off kitchenwards.

It was a square white envelope with no superscription. Sophie held it in her hand for a long time, before sliding her nail under the flap, and extracting the single sheet of paper inside.

'Sophie,' it began brusquely. 'There is nothing I can say or do which will atone for my treatment of you last night. I wish to offer you my apologies for my conduct, naturally, but in addition I feel it would be best for us both if we were to seek a legal separation. Unfortunately I have to be away for several weeks, but when I return I will give the necessary instructions to my lawyers. In the meantime, I suggest you return to your parents' home in England, and I have told my secretary to supply you with plane reservations and money. Naturally, you may offer John and your mother any explanation you please, and I will support whatever you say.'

She stared at it blankly. Signed, she noticed, with his initials as if it was some internal memo, instead of his personal warrant for heartbreak.

A moan rose in her throat, and she sank down on the rug, crumpling the paper in her hand.

She was still sitting there staring in front of her a few minutes later when Luica came in with a tray of coffee.

'There has been a 'phone call, *Signora*, from the bank. A messenger is bringing you plane tickets and other papers. I did not understand.' She frowned. 'Are you going on a trip, *Signora*? Do you wish me to pack for you?'

Sophie forced her pallid lips into a smile. 'It's—only just been decided, Lucia. The *Signor* thought as he's going to be away for some time, that I might like to go and stay with my mother.'

Luica beamed. 'Always so good, so thoughtful of others, even as a child. It will be good for you, *Signora*, to be with your mother again.'

Under normal circumstances, yes, Sophie thought forlornly, as she swallowed some coffee past the agonising lump in her throat. But not when she was being—sent back like an unwanted gift.

She could imagine it all—the surprise and pleasure when she first arrived, then the tactful questions, and the ultimate distress.

Besides, what could she possibly say to them.

'I love him more than life itself, but I never told him so, and anyway it wouldn't have been enough to stop him kicking me out of his bed.'

She replaced the coffee cup in its saucer with an angry rattle. Plane tickets could be provided, but that didn't mean they had to be used. She had her own passport, and she could go anywhere—as long as anywhere was a tiny island not so many miles from Capri.

She caught her breath at the simplicity of it. Avirenze was where it had begun, and Avirenze was where she would fight to keep him, even if it took the rest of their lives together.

'*Signora* Marchese,' Dr Lorenzo's tones were pleading. 'This is an isolated spot in winter. I am sure, under the circumstances, your husband would wish you to move to the mainland.'

Sophie gave him a mischievous smile. 'Then I'm very glad he's still in the Middle East,' she retorted. 'I like it here, and you've admitted yourself that I'm perfectly healthy. In fact, apart from a slight queasiness in the mornings, I never felt better.'

The doctor shook his head at her chidingly. 'But with your first child—and so very early in the pregnancy—it would be better to take no risks.'

'I don't intend to,' Sophie assured him, laying a protective hand across her abdomen. 'I lead a very quiet life here.'

'I am aware of that,' Dr Lorenzo said repressively. 'We all do at this time of year. But I am surprised that you choose to be here for so long a time alone—even spending Christmas without company.'

'Well, I had company, although I didn't know it,' Sophie said lightly. She gave him a wicked look. 'Last time you suspected I was pregnant, *dottore*, you were wrong. Aren't you glad to have your diagnosis confirmed this time.'

Dr Lorenzo grimaced. 'I had hoped you would have forgotten that, *Signora*. I am afraid you were not pleased with me then.'

'But after the news you've given me today, I'd forgive you anything,' she laughed.

'And when will you tell Angelo the good news?'

Sophie paused. 'Why—just as soon as I can.'

Dr Lorenzo smiled at her. 'I can imagine his pride and delight, *Signora*.' He hesitated. 'Perhaps I should not say this to you—or perhaps you already know it, but his has been a lonely life in many ways. I have seen him grow from a young child during his visits to Avirenze, and always he was a solitary figure.'

'Solitary,' Sophie protested. 'With the Marchese clan around him?'

The doctor sighed. 'But he was born to be the leader, *Signora*. It set him apart from an early age. He has always been my friend, but I can say truthfully I have never envied him.' He patted her hand. 'But now that he has a wife to love him, and a child to look forward to in the summer, he need never be lonely again, and I am happy for him.'

Sophie found the doctor's words coming back to her over and over again, as she took her usual walk through the gardens and down to the cove that afternoon.

Was that aloof quality she had so much resented merely the outward manifestation of a loneliness which had inhibited Angelo since his childhood. Perhaps that was why he had spent so much time at Bishop's Wharton in former years, to try and capture for himself some of the warmth of their family life. And maybe he had asked Sophie to marry him because he had subconsciously sought to transfer some of that warmth to his own bleakly glamorous environment.

If that was so, then she had failed him badly, she thought sombrely. She'd always been conscious of her own doubts, uncertainties and inhibitions, rarely considering if he could be suffering in the same way.

It had been the glamour which had frightened her, she admitted candidly to herself. That had made it easy for her to mask her jealousy of the other women in his life as dislike and contempt. Perhaps even Mark had been a smokescreen to hide the feelings for Angelo she did not dare acknowledge even to herself.

She paused and looked at the grove of cypresses where the garden house had stood. That had been the only shock of her visit. Vittorio had welcomed her almost tearfully, and installed her with due ceremony in the tapestry suite, where Angelo had taken her after she'd discovered Mark and Vanessa together. But on her first exploration of the grounds she had noticed the garden house was missing, the site where it had stood completely cleared. When she had asked Vittorio what had become of it, he looked faintly embarrassed.

'The *Signor* ordered its complete removal, *Signora*. He felt the sight of it might remind you of past—unhappiness.'

'That was thoughtful of him,' she said calmly. 'But there was no need to go to those lengths. Its being there wouldn't have worried me.'

And it was the truth. Perhaps Angelo had been right when he'd said that Mark's betrayal had hurt her pride more than her heart. Oh, she'd been in love with him, for a while. It would be unjust to herself to pretend anything else. But Angelo was, and always had been her love, and it was tragic she had taken so long to recognise it—and admit it.

One day they would build something else on the site of the garden house. A little summer pavilion, she thought smiling, where she could sit with her needlepoint while the children played. And Angelo would leave his everlasting paperwork and walk across the lawns to be with her.

She turned to go back to the house, and stopped dead, her eyes widening incredulously. Was her imagination playing her tricks, or was he actually standing there watching her?

She took a couple of eager steps forward, then faltered, deterred by the bleak hostility of his gaze.

She said, 'No-one told me you were coming. Did they tell you where to find me?'

His voice was bitter. 'They did not have to tell me, Sophie. Once Vittorio told me you were staying here, I guessed for myself where you would be. Can't you tear yourself away from the place even now? As for why I am here, it was an impulse. An impulse which I now regret.' He paused. 'I thought you were in England. I gave instructions . . .'

'I know you did,' Sophie agreed coolly. 'And I ignored them.'

'That is evident,' he said wearily. 'But it need make no difference. Allow me some time for a meal, and a shower, and I will take the boat back to the mainland this evening.'

'Then you'd better have your shower as quickly as possible,' Sophie said brightly. 'Shall I turn on the water for you?'

His mouth tightened. 'Don't play games, Sophie. I am not in the mood.' He turned and started back towards the villa and she caught him up. He glanced at her impatiently. 'I am going to my suite,' he told her. 'And I am quite capable of finding my own way there.'

'I'm sure you are.' She smiled at him. 'But didn't Vittorio tell you that I was using it too.'

There was a grim pause. Then, 'No,' he said grittily. 'That was a detail he failed to mention. But, no matter. There are other bathrooms in other parts of the house.'

'Looking for an escape yet again, Angelo?' She threw his own challenge back at him recklessly. 'Why, what are you frightened of, I wonder?'

He turned on her almost viciously. 'Do you want to know, *Signora*? Do you really want to know what I'm frightened of? I'll tell you. I'm frightened that if I don't walk away from you I'll forget every promise I made to myself, forget my sense of decency and take you here on the ground like a whore. And do you really know why I'm here? Because, even after staying away twice as long as I need have done, you were still there in my bloodstream, haunting me day and night. I was going to England to see you, to beg you to come back to me on any terms you cared to name, and all the time I was making the reservations something in my head was nagging me to come here to Avirenze. And when I got here, and Vittorio told me you'd been living here for over two months, I couldn't believe it. It was like a miracle.' He paused. 'And then, when I found you again, you were in—that—place.' He shouted the words. 'Wanting him. Hating me. The old pattern.'

She moved to him then, standing so close she was almost touching him, aware as she did so that he was trembling.

'And now do you want to know something, *Signor*? I was not dreaming about Mark. I was planning what we could build there instead. A little summer house. I thought, rather like the folly at Bishops Wharton. Somewhere it will be cool and quiet even in the hot weather while I'm waiting for your baby.' She took his nerveless hand and put it on her body. 'He's too small to kick, but he's here just the same, under my heart.' She slid her arms up round his neck, a smile trembling on her lips. 'Oh, darling,' she whispered. 'Why did you stay away so long? I love you so much, and I want you so terribly.' She drew his head down and kissed him on the mouth, her lips lingering sensuously, her tongue stroking along the curve of his lower lip. 'But it's too cold and damp on the ground,' she added pressing little kisses to his face and throat. 'I think the baby and I would prefer to go indoors at this time of year.'

His arms went round her gently at first, then more fiercely until he was almost crushing the breath from her body, and lifting her off the ground so that she was forced to cling to him, laughing. Then hand in hand, they ran together to the house.

But inside the privacy of the tapestry suite, Angelo seemed to hesitate, to draw back.

She put her arms round him. 'Is something wrong? Don't you want me?'

'More than my own life,' he said unsteadily. 'But I'm not accustomed to so many miracles all at once. And besides——' he paused, his face agonised with indecision. 'Might it not hurt the baby.'

They were still in the *salotto*. Sophie smiled and sank down on to the carpet, tugging him gently down beside her. 'This baby is going to have to grow accustomed to his father making love to his mother. 'She took his hands and placed them on the buttons closing the front of her dress. 'Now, don't you think you've kept me waiting long enough, *mia amante*?'

He said huskily, 'Too long. Ah, Sophie, my love, my heart's desire . . .'

His hands fumbled the buttons, as clumsy and vulnerable as a boy with his first love, and tenderly she helped him, and then unfastened his own clothes. He took her slowly, almost reve rently, and she could have wept at the painful sweetness of their coming together. They moved gently, and she cradled his face in her hands, watching the strain and the tension melt from him, feeling the urgency mount in them both until they were overtaken, overwhelmed by the passion of their need for each other.

Light years later, he said, 'I could sleep for a week.'

'Then you shall.' Sophie stroked the dark head pillowed on her breasts.

'But only if you sleep with me,' he added, sending her a lazy grin.

'Of course.' She paused. 'Shall we stay here, or would you be more comfortable in bed?'

'I shall never in my life be more comfortable than I am at this minute.' He turned his head slightly and let his mouth caress one warm, rosy-tipped mound. 'You see? Everything I most need within reach.'

There was a little silence, then she said shyly, 'Am I truly that, Angelo? As you called me—your heart's desire?'

'Yes, beloved, although I did not realise it at first, even though I had always planned to marry you someday.' He paused. 'Then you came to me that day in London, and told me you wanted to marry Mark, and I had this sudden violent reaction, and realised that for the first time in my life I was actually jealous over a woman. It was a shattering experience for me. And then I kissed you, *carissima*, and I knew then that no power on earth was going to make me give you up.'

He lifted himself on to one elbow and looked

down at her. He said quietly. 'But there is something you must know, Sophie, although it may hurt you a little.' He paused. 'Your—Mark made it clear to me that he was for sale the first time I met him at your parents' anniversary dinner. He had already given John the same impression which will explain his hostility to him.' He shrugged. 'John, of course, could have paid him off, but I felt as head of the family it was my duty. I asked him to Avirenze, not to trap him, but to discuss the terms under which he would relinquish you completely.' His mouth tightened. 'It has to be said that at once he made my task easier by getting heavily into debt at bridge. But he embarked on his—adventure with Vanessa for reasons entirely his own. I think,' he added slowly, 'that she may have given him the false impression that I was his rival for her favours, and this whetted his appetite where she was concerned.'

'So, when we met in New York, almost everything he said was a lie,' Sophie said. 'But why?'

Angelo shrugged again. 'He was always an opportunist. I imagine he saw an opportunity to make trouble between us. He knew, of course, that I would wish to protect you from the truth about him.'

Sophie bit her lip. 'Did he never care for me at all?' she said in a small voice. 'Was it only ever the money?'

He smiled into her eyes. 'No, at first he wanted you for yourself *mia cara*. What man would not? But when he found out your family connections then greed took over.' He paused again. 'When Fabrizio told me you'd seen him—talked to him for a long time—I didn't know what to expect. I—thought you still cared for him. That he might try and get you back.' He shook his head. 'When I came back to the apartment, I was half crazy with jealousy and worry. All those long months of trying to be patient, of hoping that eventually you would need my lovemaking, even if you didn't want my love, only to have him walk back into your life.' He was silent for a long moment. He said, 'I was—desperate, *carissima*—and that was why . . .' There was pain in the dark eyes, and his mouth was taut suddenly. 'Sophie, I have to know. The baby—was it *that* night that we . . .?'

She put up a hand and touched his cheek with infinite tenderness. 'I think so.'

He sighed deeply, shudderingly. 'I—wish it had been different.'

Sophie shook her head slowly, smiling at him. 'I don't. At least that night taught me that you were human. I'd begun to wonder.' She hesitated. 'You were always—remote before then. Even when we were closest I felt it was—a duty you were trying to get over with as quickly as possible.' She gave him a shy look. 'I'd never been sure, you see, that you really wanted me. I thought perhaps that I was suitable wife material but—dull.'

'You thought that?' He sounded genuinely amazed. '*Carissima*, there was not a night of our married life when I did not ache to hold you in my arms and—worship you.' His mouth twisted wrily. 'But you only seemed to—suffer my attentions, not welcome them, so—I held back, hoping that one night you would turn to me.'

'But I did,' she protested. 'The night I brought you the unicorn—I thought then, but . . .' She swallowed. 'You made it—wonderful for me, but then you—stopped, and I didn't know why.'

He said gently, 'Because I saw you were crying, and I thought it was because you were in my arms, and not his. Besides,' he added wrily. 'You were only there in my bed, *carissima*, because you thought that if you continued to withold yourself from me, I might go to Nicole, or some other woman. Isn't that true?'

She flushed a little. 'Well, perhaps, she was the catalyst, but she wasn't the only reason I was there. And I tried to let you know that I was willing . . .'

He dropped a kiss on the tip of her nose. 'I remember it well, *mia cara*. You sounded like a reluctant hostess offering an unwelcome guest a second helping. Besides,' he added drily. 'I was tied up in knots over you, and I was not at all sure I was capable of treating you gently, or with any kind of consideration. It seemed better to wait.' He smiled in self-derision. 'I had—various plans for the following day, but when I got back from Nassau, you were almost hostile. I could only assume you were regretting the previous night, and it would be fatal to rush you into the kind of intimacy you were not ready for.' He took her face in his hands. 'Why did you treat me like that, *carissima*?'

Sohpie bit her lip. 'I was disappointed because

you'd gone out. And it occurred to me you might have gone to see that night club singer—make some excuse for not having followed up the invitation she gave you during her performance,' she added unhappily.

Angelo stared at her incredulously. 'You thought—that?' He sighed. 'But then, why not? The good God knows I had never given you much cause to trust me. But I never went near her, *mia bella*, you must believe that. I went into Nassau to buy you a present. 'He gave her a rueful look. 'But when next we met, the gift seemed—inappropriate, so I told myself I'd been a fool, and put it away.'

'Oh.' Sophie looked at him remorsefully. 'I'm sorry, darling . . .'

He kissed her and sat up. 'No more apologies, *cara*. We can waste too much precious time on recriminations, when all that matters is that we are together, and that we love each other. And I still have your present,' he added, reaching for his discarded jacket. 'I have carried it with me ever since, as a good luck token, even when there seemed no hope for us.'

He produced a small jewellers' case from an inside pocket and handed it to her.

Sophie opened it, and gasped. A white jade unicorn, exquisitely fragile, and suspended from a thin gold chain lay inside.

She looked at him starrily. 'It's beautiful.'

'There's a shop on Bay Street which specialises in such things,' he said. 'I had seen it days before, and decided I would buy it for you before we left Nassau.' He paused. 'Are you going to wear it?'

Sophie's eyes danced wickedly. 'When I'm like this?' she protested.

'I can imagine no more beautiful setting,' he said, fastening the chain round her slender throat, and letting the tiny pendant slide enticingly into the valley between her naked breasts. He drew an unsteady breath. 'I had dreamed how it might look on you, my lovely one, but the reality is—devastating.' He added more soberly, 'And I have a confession, *carissima*.'

'I know,' she said swiftly. 'The other unicorn is broken. I—I found the pieces after you left on your trip.'

He sighed. 'I will not pretend it was an accident, Sophie. I was hating myself—despising myself for the way I'd treated you. I could not even face you again, and I told myself I had smashed everything—destroyed any hope we might have had of a life together. I thought too what a fool I had been to hope that a little glass ornament could ever bring us together—so, I broke it.'

'It served its purpose,' Sophie said steadily. 'And we can let it become part of the past now.'

Angelo drew her slowly and gently to her feet, and kissed her.

'Now that we have the future,' he said softly. 'My beloved. My beautiful wife.'

Sophie smiled at him, her heart in her eyes. 'My heart's desire,' she whispered.

The promise of the unicorn had been fulfilled at last.

Coming Next Month in Harlequin Presents!

863 MATCHING PAIR Jayne Bauling
A lounge singer and a hotel owner are two of a kind. He chooses to live life on the surface; she feels she has no choice. Neither have been touched by love.

864 SONG OF A WREN Emma Darcy
Her friend and lodger, a terrible tease, introduces her to his family in Sydney as his "live-in lady." No wonder his brother deliberately downplays their immediate attraction.

865 A MAN WORTH KNOWING Alison Fraser
A man worth knowing, indeed! An English secretary decides that an American author is not worth getting involved with...as if the choice is hers to make.

866 DAUGHTER OF THE SEA Emma Goldrick
A woman found washed ashore on a French Polynesian island feigns amnesia. Imagine her shock when her rescuer insists that she's his wife, the mother of his little girl!

867 ROSES, ALWAYS ROSES Claudia Jameson
Roses aren't welcome from the businessman a London *pâtisserie* owner blames for her father's ruin. She rejects his company, but most of all she rejects his assumption that her future belongs with him.

868 PERMISSION TO LOVE Penny Jordan
Just when a young woman resigns herself to a passionless marriage to satisfy her father's will, the man in charge of her fortune and her fate withholds his approval.

869 PALE ORCHID Anne Mather
When a relative of his wrongs her sister, a secretary confronts the Hawaiian millionaire who once played her for a fool. She expects him to be obstructive—not determined to win her back.

870 A STRANGER'S TOUCH Sophie Weston
One-night stands are not her style. Yet a young woman cannot deny being deeply touched by the journalist who stops by her English village to recover from one of his overseas assignments.

WORLDWIDE LIBRARY IS YOUR TICKET TO ROMANCE, ADVENTURE AND EXCITEMENT

Experience it all in these big, bold Bestsellers— Yours exclusively from WORLDWIDE LIBRARY WHILE QUANTITIES LAST

To receive these Bestsellers, complete the order form, detach and send together with your check or money order (include 75¢ postage and handling), payable to WORLDWIDE LIBRARY, to:

In the U.S.
WORLDWIDE LIBRARY
Box 52040
Phoenix, AZ
85072-2040

In Canada
WORLDWIDE LIBRARY
P.O. Box 2800, 5170 Yonge Street
Postal Station A, Willowdale, Ontario
M2N 6J3

Quant.	Title	Price
_____	**WILD CONCERTO**, Anne Mather	$2.95
_____	**A VIOLATION**, Charlotte Lamb	$3.50
_____	**SECRETS**, Sheila Holland	$3.50
_____	**SWEET MEMORIES**, LaVyrle Spencer	$3.50
_____	**FLORA**, Anne Weale	$3.50
_____	**SUMMER'S AWAKENING**, Anne Weale	$3.50
_____	**FINGER PRINTS**, Barbara Delinsky	$3.50
_____	**DREAMWEAVER**, Felicia Gallant/Rebecca Flanders	$3.50
_____	**EYE OF THE STORM**, Maura Seger	$3.50
_____	**HIDDEN IN THE FLAME**, Anne Mather	$3.50
_____	**ECHO OF THUNDER**, Maura Seger	$3.95
_____	**DREAM OF DARKNESS**, Jocelyn Haley	$3.95

	YOUR ORDER TOTAL	$_____
	New York and Arizona residents add appropriate sales tax	$_____
	Postage and Handling	$___.75
	I enclose	$_____

NAME _____

ADDRESS _____ APT.# _____

CITY _____

STATE/PROV. _____ ZIP/POSTAL CODE _____

WW3

Can you keep a secret?

You can keep this one plus 4 free novels

PASSIONATE!
CAPTIVATING!
SOPHISTICATED!

Harlequin Presents...

The favorite fiction of women the world over!

Beautiful contemporary romances that touch every emotion of a woman's heart— passion and joy, jealousy and heartache... but most of all...love.

Fascinating settings in the exotic reaches of the world— from the bustle of an international capital to the paradise of a tropical island.

All this and much, much more in the pages of

Harlequin Presents...

Wherever paperback books are sold, or through **Harlequin Reader Service**

In the U.S.	In Canada
901 Fuhrmann Blvd.	P.O. Box 2800, Postal Station A
P.O. Box 1394	5170 Yonge Street
Buffalo, NY 14240-1394	Willowdale, Ontario M2N 6J3

No one touches the heart of a woman quite like Harlequin!